Other Rhodes

Contents

Rhodes

There was someone in the airlock. Someone or something.

This wouldn't normally have been an issue, except for the fact that I was alone in the ship. We were docked in Elysium, a world in the Veiled Sisters system which was—mostly—home to a non-profit devoted to the care of seniors.

There were several cities in Elysium, large and small, where your loved ones could find comfort and solace in their final years, or, frankly, move to in the middle of their second century when modern life became difficult to cope with.

We were not docked at any of the major spaceports, those that catered to the visiting relatives or to the travels of the wealthier residents. Instead, we'd picked a small, out-of-the-way spaceport, one used by the manual laborers and repairmen and others who catered to the residents.

It was a sleepy place—I gathered most of the personnel who worked here didn't travel much—set at the edge of a small island, with just a hundred docking berths, most of which were empty.

We'd picked it precisely because it was inconspicuous. My husband, Joe Aster, was an itinerant private investigator and we were in the midst of perhaps the most difficult case of his career. He thought that keeping quiet was the best part of valor.

And I agreed, because I knew nearly nothing about the business, except what horse sense told me, and back then I'd never even seen an equine. Metaphorically or in fact.

As out of the way as we were, the chances of anyone being in the airlock were remote. Or rather, the chances of anyone being in the airlock accidentally.

Joe had been gone twenty-four hours. At the first beep from the airlock, I stopped and froze, halfway between the entrance and the stairs that led to our private quarters. I thought it was Joe coming back.

But the beeps multiplied, chaotic, and I couldn't imagine Joe missing the entry code that often. Not even if he were drunk. Or wounded.

I swallowed hard, setting the reader I'd been carrying down on the edge of the steps.

Our ship—the *West 35th Street*—was a thirdhand utility interstellar that Joe had modified to accommodate housekeeping. The bottom floor comprised the office and the kitchen. Upstairs were two sleeping rooms. There wasn't much space, and—for an interstellar—it wasn't very well-insulated against sound. Well, not sound from the airlock.

The clank, clank, and frantic beeps could be heard all over the bottom floor.

I took a deep breath, as the hair rose at the back of my neck. If it were Joe at the door, by now I'd expect to hear some of the fluent cursing for which he was known. But there was not a word.

I scurried near the door, in a bit of bravery, and punched the button for the trid pickup on the camera. It was normal for clients to arrive that way, and when they did, we usually got an eye-full of them first, before we decided to even admit them.

When I pushed the button, there was a sound like "Sfooo" and for just a second something like a grey mist showed where the 3D image of whatever was in the airlock was supposed to form.

That was it. But our camera was first class. Had to be. Tool of the trade, as Joe said. If it failed—

The hair rising at the back of my neck was joined by a feeling of cold down my spine. The only way for the camera to fail was that it had been disabled.

That meant—

That meant I was in deep trouble. You see, I am not a very large woman: all of one meter sixty-two and fifty kilos. Soaking wet. Carrying luggage. Worse, I wasn't trained in any form of fighting. That was Joe's pidgin, part of his private investigator training.

As far as I did anything for the business, it was typing and very good bookkeeping.

I had the briefest and most futile flash of anger at Joe. He was supposed to be here. He was supposed to protect me.

But it was nonsense, of course. He tried to protect me, but his job was hazardous, and he had to do his job.

On the edge of the anger came acceptance. Well, then. Joe had left me something to protect me, an equalizer, the type of weapon that could make even a small, slim woman the equal of anyone.

It was in the third drawer of my desk in the office. A small zapper that fit in my hand: one of the curious weapons we'd retrieved from Kyre ruins and Kyre technology.

Joe said it wasn't actually a ray gun, and it didn't fire energy rays. Fine. Whatever it was and whatever it did, I knew—had practiced with it enough—it had enough power and generated enough heat to fry whatever it was aimed at twenty feet off. It was one of the reasons Joe had given it to me. He said unlike projectile weapons, it was effective even against humans in armor or most kinds of mechanized attackers.

It was also illegal in most planets of the human sphere. But that was quite beside the point. Joe had explained—and I agreed—that it was better to be alive to be arrested.

So, with the background sounds of beep, beep, beep, followed by curious bangs which gave the impression of something very large and very hard bumping around in there, I turned and ran for the office.

I'd only just reached into the drawer and grabbed the little yellow weapon, when a voice came over the com from the airlock, almost making me jump out of my skin. "Stella?"

It was a strange voice, grinding and mechanical, and I took a deep breath. All right. So, the audio part of the pickups in the airlock worked.

Gun in hand, I returned to the entrance hall, just off the airlock.

There the noises—bang, bump, knock, beeeeep—were deafening, being on the other side of an airtight door. I pushed the com button and said, "Stella who?"

There was a pause in the sounds, an impression that the person—thing?—was thinking, and then, the same grinding, faintly mechanical voice: "Stella D'Or, of course."

The name seemed familiar, with that feeling I would know it if my heart weren't pounding deafeningly in my ears. But I knew one thing for sure. "She's not here."

Pause. "She must be."

"She isn't."

Something much like a scream, if you can imagine a scream emitted by an assemblage of gears and mechanical apparatus: "She must be."

Beep, bomp, crash. And then beep, beep, beep, with a will, as though whoever—whatever?—had remembered the code.

I could run forward and press the override on the door. But if it slammed open while I was there, I'd be within reach of the intruder. Or I could—

I stepped back very fast, holding the gun, pointed at the airlock's sliding door. I stood at the door to the office.

And the door slid open.

How do I describe the intruder? To begin with, he wasn't human. To continue with, he was mechanical.

He was made of some gleaming material, and six feet tall. Perfect features had been molded into the material, the kind that put the images we inherited from classical Greece to shame. Lights gleamed blue on either side of its nose, where eyes should be. There were no visible joints in molded legs or arms, or shoulders, but it bent and walked as a human, even if more stiffly, like a young child only learning the art.

A borg. My ship home had been invaded by a borg.

Borgs, common parlance for cyborgs, were even more illegal than my gun. Monstrous creatures consisting of a human brain and a robotic body, they were forbidden in every human world, even though it was rumored that the Qan Empire had long since borged all its subjects and only created new brains when the old ones wore out.

The main reason for borgs being forbidden was humanitarian.

Few borgs were created with voluntary acquiescence of the brain donor. Most people whose brains were used for that purpose had been kidnapped, killed, their brains taken by force.

And most of them didn't survive the process. Their brain just didn't find its way to the neuro-mechanical linkages of the borg body. They never recovered consciousness.

Those were the lucky ones.

Most of those who survived just couldn't communicate or move the body, and were forever entombed in the mechanical creature. Their makers usually disposed of the brain then, to make way for a new one.

Of the twenty percent or so that made it and learned to move and communicate, most were hopelessly insane. Maybe five percent adapted enough to their circumstances to be able to function.

Those five percent made the process worth it to those who needed borgs badly enough to flout the laws. Because there were planets too inhospitable to humans to be mined, occupations too difficult for humans to accomplish. And those who made money for such things simply didn't care.

Which was why the laws—including the one that said anyone finding a borg and not destroying it was an accomplice to borging, and was to be executed—had no teeth. Because sufficiently insistent demand will get supply, not matter how difficult it is to arrange. Joe had said a vast network of shadowy corporations and governments pretended to see nothing while borging went on. All the law could do was keep it small-scale.

And now you're asking, given all this: why didn't I fry the creature as soon as it came in the front hall? The zapper could do it. It was part of the reason Joe had picked it. It would cook the brain inside that glassteel carapace, before it could harm me.

I wanted to. I was going to. I pointed my zapper at it.

And it said, its voice infused with extreme relief, "Stella, there you are!"

I swallowed hard, before I could find my voice, and my finger didn't seem to obey me when I told it to push the zapper trigger. There was something very familiar to the accent and the way the words were said, if not to the voice. I couldn't have shot, right then, to save my life. Instead, my own voice sounded raspy and odd as I asked, "Who are you?"

It— He smiled, and the smile too was familiar, horribly and heartbreakingly familiar. "I'm Nick, Stella. How can you not remember me, Nick Rhodes? We work together."

I remembered Nick Rhodes. And that was the problem. Because neither Nick nor Stella nor, in fact, the address after which our ship was named existed.

They were all part of a mersi to which my husband was addicted.

My throat was now so tight that I could not speak. Nor resist. The thing walked towards the office door, gaining a sort of ease in its movement, and I scurried out of the way as it walked all the way past my desk and to the large, wood desk that Joe used to impress clients.

When it lowered itself into Joe's chair, the poor abused seat creaked like it would break, but it held fast. The seat held fast as it reclined back, turned its now low-burning blue lights towards me. The baffling smile moved across the sculpted features.

And then it put its big, sculpted feet on the desk.

Just like my husband always did. And I had a very bad feeling, one I could not quite tell myself was just a nightmare.

The Airlock Chimes

It all started as most of our cases started, with a chime from outside the airlock of our ship: a client to see Joe.

My name was Lilly Aster nee Gilden. I'd married Joe Aster three years before. Since then, we worked together. I'd joined in his business in the sense that I acted as his receptionist, accountant and general office help, as he went from world to world solving the common but not inconsequential puzzles and problems of private people for moderate fees.

Whether a woman wanted to know if that hot asteroid cowboy courting her was already married in a dozen other worlds, a father wanted to check on the mode of life of offspring who had moved to Far Itravine and never communicated, or a businessman needed to figure out if his small but plucky enterprise was being used to launder money from the Ivory Empire, Joe Aster was the man to call.

Joe had a few self-imposed restrictions on what he would and would not do. He stayed away from divorce cases, because it was easy to sink an untold amount of time in investigation and then have the client decide to reconcile and never pay. He also stayed away from murder cases, because—he said—they tended to be complicated and keep him for too long in a single world. But also, because it could get you crosswise with jurisdictions where murder was protected by custom or affiliation, by ethnic or national right.

We didn't know it, but that chime at the outer door of our spaceship would change everything. If there are inflection points in our lives, events and times after which nothing will ever be the same, this was one of them.

Our ship was docked in a regional spaceport outside the obscure city of Nysa, in a world called Pycontero, in the Seven Spinners system. We'd just finished a lucrative case, even if the client had left in tears because—

Never mind. The client had left. We were in the office, which was arguably the most luxuriously furnished room in our thirdhand interstellar, and by far the best decorated. Mostly because it was important to project stability and permanence to clients.

My desk was to the right of the door, as you go in, and it was a wood desk—Joe insisted—into the top of which the tridcomp has been built in such a way that it didn't show at all when not activated. That morning, I'd just pushed the button to activate it, and set my hands on the desktop, ready to type.

My otherwise fairly useless education had left me with impeccable typing and accounting abilities. I looked at Joe, who sat behind his vast, polished wood desk, his chair reclined back, his blue eyes staring at the ceiling as though it contained something amazing and unfathomable. For the record, it didn't. It was just silver glassteel, the only part of the room we hadn't bothered disguising as more traditional materials.

"What do I bill for?" I asked again.

"The usual," he said, staring at the ceiling.

"But Joe, we had five different interstellar calls and—"

"The usual," he said, with finality. And then, with a deep sigh, as he took his feet off the desk and sat up straight, "I hate it when things end badly for the client."

I didn't say anything, because, well... What could you do when your investigations led you to inform your client that she wasn't *precisely* legally married and, in fact, that the man she thought she had married didn't exist, but was a construct flitting from world to world and taking wealthy widows for all he could get?

"Ever think that there has to be a better way to make a living, love?" Joe asked very softly.

And the door chimed, saving him from a sharp reply.

I got up and took a turn left out of the office, to the hall where the controls of the ship squawker were.

I didn't want to answer Joe, anyway. There was no payload in it. Sure, there were a million other ways to make a living, but either they tied us to some backworld, or they required training which neither of us had.

My assets were a face—not ugly—a body—not unattractive—beautiful manners and a mastery of most fashionable dances. Throw in typing and accounting and it didn't amount to much. As for Joe, he was a trained and licensed investigator. Expensive training and lucrative, but it meant he knew a lot of laws pertaining to private investigation and privacy in various worlds and was licensed to poke his nose in other people's affairs. Add to that a natural charm of manner and a brilliant mind, and he was good at the PI business. You could say he'd been born to it.

I sympathized with his feeling of being dragged through the underbelly of the galaxy, and his occasional wish to do something else. But this is what we were, and the skills we had. What did he think we could do? Gengineering? Time Geometry?

My voice still frosty over my husband's blue-sky dreaming, I slapped the squawker on and said, "Joe Aster Investigations. How may we help you?"

There was a hesitation, and I thought I'd frightened some poor spaceport worker come to confirm our date of departure, and then a polite, rich voice that sounded familiar said, "I wish to speak to Mr. Aster. I...I might have a job for him."

Right. As per protocol, I slapped the trid viewer and a hologram of our caller formed, just inside the door between the hall and the airlock.

And I jumped back. You'd have, too. No, there was nothing horrific about the client. He was a jovial-looking, middle-aged man, maybe on the leeside of eighty, hair going white and of the kind that will fluff out, giving one a halo, grey eyes full of bonhomie and a round, reddish face. It was the rubicund countenance that smiled out at viewers throughout the Galaxy from trid broadcasts while explaining some point of culture or history, whenever the News Aggregators needed to trot a learned person onto their cast sets.

Yes, Gulbahar Felix. *That* Gulbahar Felix. He wore a casual grey suit and managed to look both amiable and hesitant. Oh, also worried, as though he had some great concern on his mind.

But perhaps I read more on his countenance than others would have. You see, he was a friend of the family, and I'd known him since I could toddle around my father's house. He'd always been *Uncle Gul* to me. I had no idea how he felt about me, since Dad had disowned me for marrying Joe. Or perhaps putting it that way was doing Daddy an injustice. After all, he'd said he'd disown me if I married Joe, and we'd registered our union in the Galactic archive that same day. So, you could say it was a choice, and I'd disowned myself.

As for Uncle Gul—I wondered if he'd been sent by Dad to take me back home. But that made no sense. For one, Dad, who owned most of Elfenheim in the Seer system, could get people much more adept at such operations than an absent-minded academic. For another...well, I knew Uncle Gul, and he didn't look like he was hiding anything. More like he was really, really worried.

I decided to chance it. First because, when Joe got in the mood to contemplate other ways of making a living, he could spend weeks reading up on jobs and possible training before he got back to actually, you know, earning money.

And second because I had no idea at all what Uncle Gul would be doing here, so far from New Oxford where he made his home. And I was curious.

I pushed the button that opened the airlock, saying, "Please come in."

As he stepped in, I closed the outer lock and opened the inner one. The precaution wasn't needed in Pycontero, whose atmosphere was almost an exact match for Earth's, but I'd learned early that living shipboard was all about habits. Breaking them might mean a fatal mistake at another time.

When I opened the inner door, it was Uncle Gul's turn to do a double take. He stood between the two retracting halves of the door, looking at me as though he were seeing a ghost. And while I'll admit that I had let my beauty regime go somewhat—I didn't have an army of beauticians to apply creams or makeup—and was wearing a casual grey one-piece, I hadn't changed enough to cause that reaction.

I smiled back at him. "Hello, Uncle Gul."

He behaved as if he had gone blind. He put his hand forward, as if he needed to touch me, to make sure I was there, but dropped his hand before touching me. "Lilly!" he said. He sounded shocked. "What are you doing here?"

My smile widened. I couldn't help it. "I live here," I said. "In the ship. I'm Mrs. Joseph Aster."

Uncle Gul's mouth dropped open. The door started beeping, because he stood in between the two halves that wanted to close. He gave himself a little shake, as though waking up, stepped forward, and snapped his mouth shut. The door closed behind him. "Well. Well. Your father said you'd married a fortune hunter, a gigolo, a man of no account. Not Joe Aster."

I felt that slight twinge I always fought when Joe was in one of his blue-sky *what can I find to do that's better?* periods. Had I married a man of no account?

Look, it's nonsense. What's more, I know it's nonsense. If Joe had wanted to marry me for my money, he wouldn't have gone ahead when I told him that if he married me, my father would cast me off with the clothes on my body.

What's more, if he'd married me because he thought Daddy would relent, he'd have divorced me when Daddy didn't. Instead, he'd told me again and again that he needed only me. And hadn't even acted upset when all I could do for the business was typing and accounting. I was more upset about that than he was. But still, now and then the twinge came up, that feeling like I'd put my foot down on what should be solid ground, and it wouldn't hold me.

"Well, Lilly," Uncle Gul said. "You know what your father is."

"I do, Uncle Gul."

He seemed...hesitant.

"My husband really is a very good investigator," I said.

"Oh, I know. I know. Famous for it," Uncle Gul said. "That's why I never thought... But you see, I'm not sure..."

"If you speak to him," I said. "He can tell you whether or not he wishes to take the case. He's very good at judging where we can help and where we can't."

"Well... Yes, it's just... It might be very dangerous," Uncle Gul said.

"We've taken dangerous cases before," I said. And it was true, though to be fair, we'd never taken a case we *knew* would be dangerous. What usually happened was that we thought we were investigating a common grifter or swindler and suddenly found ourselves facing an armed spaceship on attempting to dock, or perhaps a madman shooting pellet guns at us while we were out for dinner.

Uncle Gul frowned and compressed his lips.

I moved ahead, and opened the door to the office. "If you'd come in, Doctor Gulbahar Felix."

I was aware, by the corner of my eye, of Joe taking his feet off the desk, sitting upright and snapping me a startled look.

I didn't have time for that. Both Joe and Uncle Gul were acting hesitant. I decided to give neither the opportunity to weasel out of business.

It worked on Uncle Gul, too. Perhaps because the way I said it was so official and like I expected him to follow through, he bowed his head to me, just a little more than a nod, said, "Thank you," and walked past me and into the office.

When I went in, he was advancing on Joe, hand extended, and there was nothing for it but for Joe to stand up and offer his hand in return, for one of his patented firm handshakes and reassuring smile. "Doctor Gulbahar Felix," my husband said, sounding stunned. I could almost see his eyebrow twitch, as he longed to raise it at me.

Uncle Gul smiled as he shook Joe's hand and said, "Mr. Aster." He stepped back and dropped into the comfortable red armchair that faced Joe's desk squarely. There were five other chairs and even a sofa against the wall, and at various times we'd used every seat available in the office so that we could accommodate groups of clients. But the red chair was the logical seat for a single client. I took my place behind my desk and pushed the button that made my holo-screen private, so only someone sitting where I sat could see it.

I didn't know if Joe would want me to stay and take notes. Sometimes clients preferred if I left. But procedure was for me to stay unless told to leave.

"You come highly recommended, Mr. Aster," Uncle Gul said. "My friend Velibor Magro said you helped him track down the missing cargo on his— Well, his missing cargo. And my friend Alcides Carson said you plugged the data leaks in his enterprise back in Emia."

Joe actually blushed. The fact that Uncle Gul had picked not just two of our most famous clients, but also two of the most difficult cases Joe had solved was flattering, of course, but Joe's embarrassment also probably had something to do with the fact that it was Uncle Gul saying it.

For a moment they sat, looking at each other. It was normal. The client was evaluating Joe, and Joe was evaluating the client. The client's evaluation of Joe mattered, of course, because the last thing you wanted was an unwilling client. Evaluating a client was part of the skills at which Joe excelled and which he'd taught me.

But in this case, my acumen was blunted by familiarity. I'd grown up with Uncle Gul, so I wasn't absolutely sure what Joe would make of him, nor even if just being familiar with Uncle Gul from a thousand holo transmissions made it hard to evaluate the man now. I knew what Uncle Gul saw, though.

My love for Joe was new enough that it was easy to remember what first impression he made: Uncle Gul saw a tall man, with lean features, a mop of blond hair, and direct, clear blue eyes. Joe had been dressed to see the previous client, in a one-piece suit in startling blue, which was all the fashion in this part of the galaxy. He looked professional, intelligent and eager. The puzzled look he cast me was the only crack in the façade.

Uncle Gul must have decided Joe was trustworthy. You could tell from the way he leaned back in the red chair and folded his hands over his stomach. "I have...a puzzle," he said.

"We like puzzles," Joe said, and smiled at me. "Don't we, Lil?" His eyes still posed a question, the question being why I'd let the client in without warning.

I nodded and kept my gaze as blank as I knew how.

Uncle Gul frowned. "This one..." He splayed his hands on his thighs, as though trying to assure himself of solidity and reality. "Well, this one is either a mare's nest, or it will be very difficult." He made a face. "I'd pay you in either case, of course. But if it turns out to be... Well, it could be life-endangering. It might also blow up some of the biggest— It could go very high up."

The startled look came and went in Joe's eyes. It wasn't that we hadn't heard similar warnings from other clients, but it must have seemed strange to get it from a gentle Academician like Uncle Gul. Joe leaned forward, in an attitude of perfect attention.

Uncle Gul sighed. "What...what do you know about borging?" he asked.

Joe sat up and straightened his shoulders but made no sound. It left me to say in a startled voice, "But it doesn't happen, does it? It's just a horror story, right?"

I saw Joe shake his head minimally, while Uncle Gul turned to look at me full-on, then said, "Perhaps... Er... Perhaps Lilly shouldn't be here for this discussion?"

"No," Joe said. "She stays." Which is the reason he'd had me get a first-level investigator license. It actually didn't qualify me to investigate anything—we didn't have the money for the full training, much less for not working for the year I was taking the training—but it allowed me to know details of his investigations.

"Hardly the proper—"

"She's my partner. She stays. If she leaves, I'll just have to tell her everything later."

Uncle Gul looked doubtful. "Well, if you're sure."

"I'm sure." He told Uncle Gul all he knew about borging, from the battery tech found in Kyre ruins, to the materials like glassteel, and how it allowed everything from tiny guns to...borging.

Uncle Gul inclined his head. It wasn't so much a nod, as though bowing under the weight of things he didn't want to think about or admit.

Then he looked up. "Well, if this isn't a nightmare conjured up by my imagination, it is a borging case. What's more, for the borging to go on, it would require the cooperation of several Galactic oversight boards, and what is supposed to be at least one humanitarian organization.

"If you take this case, you'll be going up against some of the most dangerous and powerful people in the Galaxy."

Uncle Gul

Uncle Gul spilled it. Altogether, it was almost nothing, and I was inclined to agree with him that it was all a nightmare.

Uncle Gul's friend, an older but less successful academic, Narkissus Humel, had retired a few years ago.

Because of the costs of living in New Oxford, most retiring academics moved out of that

world. Narkissus had looked around long and hard for a place to live out his golden years. Because of his age, nearing the middle of his second century, he thought he might need assistance with everyday tasks soon, so he'd picked a planet, Elysium, which was run by the West Islands Organization, a charity that devoted itself to keeping elderly people comfortable and happy to the end and took only nominal payments.

"I hear it's a beautiful world, much like Earth, but going through a warmer phase, so its climate ranges from moderate to tropical, with no true frigid zones," Uncle Gul said. "And it's been cultivated like a garden. People, from the end of their first century on, may choose to live there, and they have all kinds of housing, from cities, where people get to live independently, to skilled nursing facilities, if they require specialized care." He pursed his lips. "I visited with Narkissus when he went to give it a look-over. He asked me to. I saw nothing wrong with it. Beautiful place. I thought I might very well consider it when my time came. So Narkissus moved there—"

He took a deep breath. "Narkissus said— He sent me something. Well, he sent me many recorded messages and letters. He was very happy there for some months, but after about six months, he said that he suspected there was something wrong. The pattern of deaths was wrong, he said. People were dying who were in better shape and younger than others."

"But that happens, doesn't it?" Joe asked. "I mean, mere happenstance. No one has ever been able to quantify the dying process or eliminate uncertainty in the human lifespan."

"Sure. But he thought there was too much happenstance going around to be *mere*. I think he decided to investigate. He used to be a professor of criminal jurisprudence. The last message I got from him indicated that he suspected something big was going on... And then communication stopped."

"Where does borging come in?" Joe asked.

Uncle Gul shook his head. "It comes afterwards," he said. "When I tried to investigate what had happened to Narkissus, I was just told he had died unexpectedly. No details. When I visited, no one could tell me what had happened. All his records were lost." He paused a long time. "I decided to leave. There was nothing to do. I suspected incompetence, not malice. I assumed that someone had failed in taking care of Narkissus, not that there was anything nefarious. But when I got on my ship, it had been tampered with." He seemed to anticipate our arguing with him on that.

"I'm quite sure," he said. "I set a course, but it took another." He shrugged. "I can't prove it, but I think it was designed to make me either precipitate into the system's sun, or perhaps just end up in space, unable to do an interstellar jump or com anyone." He gave a sudden feral grin. "They didn't know that I was a pilot in long-haul courses in my youth. It's not the normal occupation for someone who becomes a mind-worker. But it's how I earned money for my education. So I fixed the drive, and the autopilot, but not so fast that I didn't come dangerously close to the sun and the world closest to it. A place where no ship would go that didn't have to. I swear to you, though I can't prove it, that there were borgs working on that surface. I couldn't get more than a glimpse as I was trying to save my ship. Yes, it might have been a trick of my eyes, but there was movement and human-shaped forms. I went back to New Oxford, not sure if I hadn't just had a nightmare. And then..."

"And then?"

"And then I started investigating. The inner planet of that system does in fact have the kind of minerals used for the Kyre batteries, and cannot easily be mined by humans, but it can be mined by robots. However, every time I looked into it, talked to someone about it, every time I came close... There was an attack on me or my possessions. My house was broken into and all of Narkissus's electronic letters were erased. My house was vandalized, and a lot of my research taken. My flycar was tampered with to crash, and it could have killed me. And that convinced me—"

"That there was something criminal behind this? But surely not borging, as such? I mean—"

"I know, I know. It's why I said it might all be a nightmare. But my feeling... I had a strong feeling there was more there. And I have learned to follow my feelings."

Joe didn't say anything. He didn't have much room to say anything. He, himself, often operated on such principles.

"And so," Uncle Gul said, "I thought I'd talk to a professional about it. I asked around my circle of acquaintances, and your name kept coming up."

Joe nodded. "It won't be cheap."

"That goes without saying," Uncle Gul said. "No one who is an expert comes cheap. I... I took the liberty of bringing a credgem with me?" He got up and put it on Joe's desk.

This was, frankly speaking, dirty pool. Joe could get all philosophical about things, and he might spend some time lamenting the harsh realities of the field we made a living in. But when push came to shove, he knew we had to live, and he knew living involved money.

Money was also security, and added more time to spend daydreaming of other things he could do.

Joe picked up the gem and slid it over the hidden reader on his desk, then pushed the also-hidden mechanism that relayed it to my screen. And I blinked. A thousand Lyrs. Lyr was the one currency that didn't need to have a notation on conversion. Eurilia was to banking as New Oxford was to education. While every government in the galaxy had its own currency, Eurilia had currency that all the other currencies were pegged to. And it was based on something solid and rare, though I could no longer remember what, if I'd ever learned. All I remembered was my father talking about it being the only currency in the Galaxy worth a damn. And a thousand Lyrs... Well, you couldn't buy a mansion in Daddy's neighborhood with it. But you could buy a small home by the sea, in a very pleasant and easygoing world—say, Far Itravine—and spend the next ten years daydreaming, if you so wished.

Uncle Gul must have misread our expressions. Which made sense. I supposed in his—and my father's—world, that amount was nothing. "A down payment, of course," he said. "I presume the fee would be ten times more and whatever expenses you incur."

"Of course," Joe said, sounding as though he dealt in that kind of cash every day and twice on Sunday.

I knew him well enough to know what ran through his mind right then: this was enough money for one or both of us to get different training, or merely to settle down and live a carefree life. Perhaps, at last, time to have children. We'd both talked of children, and both of us wanted them, but it would be hard to manage on our budget and while living as itinerant investigators.

Joe got up. "I'll leave you with Lilly. Give her all pertinent facts about Mr. Humel, if you would, and I'll start the investigation. I have some important work to attend to."

I kept my face impassive, even after Joe had closed the door. But it was hard, because my husband was a rat.

Look, I didn't know for sure he wasn't working elsewhere. We had a spare room upstairs, to the side of our bedroom. And it had a tricomp which was linked to Galacticom as these were.

But we only had this one case. If Joe was going upstairs to start investigating, he probably would have waited till he had a few other facts.

No. I knew exactly what Joe was going to do—the same thing he did whenever he was tired, nervous, or restless.

You see, there was this series of mersis. They were a mystery series, set in the early twentieth century in New York City, on Earth.

Ten thousand years later, it was hard to reconstruct the city, but this series was as accurate as it could be made. Historians consulted with the creative team, and other historians talked about how amazingly accurate it was. Sometimes revisions were announced and all those who'd bought the episodes before were sent the revised ones.

It was about a detective named Rhodes, a veteran of the first Earth War. He'd been disfigured in some way and wore a ceramic mask to hide his face. He never went forth to investigate, either. That work was left to his assistant, a blond bombshell named Stella D'Or.

I'd never taken an episode, but I knew all about it, because Joe loved the stories and the world, and always told me about them.

It was hard to behave professionally and not make a face when I knew Joe would be upstairs, living an episode in our mersi machine, being some detective in a lost city in the cradle of mankind.

But I'd learned some stuff since I'd stopped being the very rich and pampered Miss Gilden. One of the things I'd learned was how to be professional even while

Joe behaved like an artiste. I smiled at Uncle Gul. "Go ahead," I said. "Tell me all you remember about Narkissus Humel."

Uncle Gul cleared his throat and spilled it all. I only had to ask a few questions, and those only because Uncle Gul didn't realize what I wanted was the deep background of Narkissus Humel, not just his background as it related to his final misadventure.

And because Uncle Gul didn't know as much about his friend as he would like. "You see, he was much older than me," Uncle Gul said. "A full-fledged professor for a good fifty years by the time I was invested. So, some of this will require quite a good deal of thought."

What he came through with at last wasn't a lot, but it was enough to start with. Narkissus Humel had been born in Guniarr, the capital city of Beccara, a world of little importance in the Flame System.

"I think his father might have been a fisherman," Uncle Gul said. "Or a dealer in fish. Something like that. Something manual, relating to fish. I remember Narkissus refused to eat fish because he said he'd had his fill of it before he grew to maturity. Even the smell annoyed him, and he used to make faces if I ordered it when we were out eating together."

He had no idea of the composition of Humel's birth family. "I think he had a brother?" he said. "And maybe a sister. But I can't be sure. It's very hard, you see, because—" Uncle Gul shrugged. "Our acquaintance and later friendship was as fellow professors in the university. We understood each other in that realm, and talked of things that were important in New Oxford. University policy, discoveries in our respective fields, perhaps a new administrator, or the changes in a restaurant down the block. So, all I know about his background are dropped references, which this far past don't immediately come to mind. Yes, I think a brother. Almost for sure a sister, but not as certain of that. It might have been a female cousin. He said something about his brother being a ship's captain once, when I was talking about my days flying interstellars."

Humel had been married twice or maybe three times, so about average. "I was the oddity, never having been brave enough to tie my life with another person's for fifty years or so," Uncle Gul said, and smiled ruefully. "It seemed too close, too exposed. Anyway, I knew Narkissus's second, or perhaps first wife well. She was the one he was married to when we became friends. A hologram artist, Idelle Zay? You might remember her; I think she visited your father once when I was there. No? Well, you might have been too young to remember. That was the last time I saw her, long after her marriage to Narkissus expired, and to be honest, I don't remember now whether she might still be alive. She was Narkissus's age or thereabouts, and so many people choose to voluntarily end it before turning one-fifty. You know, she was a lovely woman. Oh, tall and elegant, one of those slim blondes that seemed to be made out of blown glass with touches of gold. All flowing lines and sparkle. But she was lovely as a human being, too. She was a fast friend, and amusing to be around. If I'd had a little more courage... But that's neither here nor there. Anyway, their contract expired a good fifty years ago, and I don't remember if she had a new one, or what she was doing when I met her at your father's. There were so many people there, and it was such a large party we barely exchanged two words.

"After their contract expired, Narkissus married a much younger woman, probably no more than twenty-five at the time. She was like Narkissus, short and olive-skinned, with curly dark hair. Like Narkissus, too, in that she preferred not to have a very active social life. So, I saw her a lot less than I did Idelle. Instead of meeting Narkissus at his home or attending dinners and parties given by his wife, I met with him at various restaurants and clubs. Their contract expired just before he decided to go to Elysium, or at least to seek a place for his retirement."

At my prompt he shook himself. "Oh, you'll want her name, of course. That is Raine Chlo. She—" He stopped, as though startled. "You know, I don't have the slightest idea what she did for a living?"

Narkissus had no children, or at least no children that Uncle Gul had ever heard of. "I really think his life had no space for children. He was so interested in his field, you see, and spent so much time working that he barely had time for a wife." A smile broke Uncle Gul's seriousness, but for only a moment. "Well, neither did I. Which is one reason I never married, I suppose, and why Narkissus seemed to marry women who had busy lives of their own." He frowned. "It does bother me I can't remember what Raine did. I mean, she seemed busy and successful. There's a certain way women carry themselves. But I don't remember what she did. It might come to me later, and if so, I'll call you."

I agreed to this and prodded him for more facts about the—presumably dead—Narkissus. What I found out all put together didn't amount to much, or at least not much I could use for anything. For instance, I found his favorite book was *The Edge of the Knife* by Lombart Orli and that he spent his free time trying to solve past crimes. That he liked fishing, but hated hunting, despite the fact that he didn't like eating fish. That he always drank tea, not coffee, and a long list of things that really had nothing to do with anything.

I suppose when all is said and done, it's all that's left of a long friendship: a collection of little moments, shattered under the impact of time and forgetfulness, and a bagful of facts and incidents that don't amount to much at all, but which are important to an individual because they are tied to an important friendship.

I have it all saved on the tricomp. If you want to see it, and you come across me in real life sometime, ask me for it. I doubt it will be of more use to you than it was to us.

Uncle Gul looked sad as I walked him to the airlock, as though talking about his friend made him even sadder than he'd been before.

Just before he entered the airlock, he turned around, and seized hold of both my hands for a moment. "Lilly," he said. "Listen, I was serious about what I said. This might be a very difficult job, and I'll never forgive myself if something should happen to you. So... So, if it seems like you're going to get in trouble, you or that husband of yours, don't do it. Just... Just drop it. You'll be able to keep the down payment, of course. After all... Well, Narkissus is dead, and I wouldn't like it to be—" He shrugged. "You get to be my age, and you start thinking that you don't want to cause any more problems in the world. That's all."

His hands were dry like twigs, and he held a little too hard.

I managed to extricate one hand and used it to pat his hands, still holding on to my other hand, in what I hoped was a reassuring manner. "We'll be careful, Uncle Gul," I said.

And then he cycled out of the airlock and was gone. And Joe was coming down in the elevator.

Strange Findings

"You rat," I said, as I was turning around, but when I looked at Joe, he didn't look like he'd mersied an episode of Rhodes.

Instead, he looked worried, and frowned in confusion at my words. "I'm sorry?"

"I thought you'd left to mersi Rhodes."

"Oh." He shook his head. "No, I left to talk to Jim and see what he knew about Narkissus Humel."

Jim was James Brighton, an old friend of mine from my New Oxford days. A friend, never a lover, but one who had stayed my friend after what most of my world considered a most unpalatable marriage. He'd commed on the day of the wedding to give us his best wishes, and he'd stayed our friend.

Part of it was that he also knew Joe, who had worked with him in the past on some investigation or other. Jim was a mediator of news and stories. So much that was newsworthy suffused the Galaxy that it was impossible to even get the top, most important events for a single world. So, there were news mediators, and Jim was one of them.

Jim was a slim, dark man with unruly hair, who attended the same schools I did but didn't come from the same class. In fact, while I was there on Daddy's money, he was there on a scholarship because of brains and native curiosity.

He'd never left New Oxford. And, in his public persona, he seemed to have no life beyond his work. All of which didn't explain, but maybe helped him be inordinately pleased when Joe and I married. Maybe because I married outside of my social class, maybe because he thought Joe was smart. Who knows?

Later on, our friendship—as a married couple—with Jim had become closer when Joe had extricated Jim from a problem that indicated he did have a personal life, even if I couldn't figure out where he found the time for it.

"You look worried?" I said.

"Well, Jim didn't have a lot," he said. "But what he did have seems to indicate that there was no such person as Narkissus Humel."

"Oh?" I said.

"Oh," Joe repeated. "The information we have doesn't correlate to any birth records, in any of the worlds that keep birth records, and there is no indication of any such person. The extant genetic profile, run against a database of humanity for the last three hundred years, comes up dry."

"But that by itself indicates that there is something wrong," I said. "It is impossible for someone to live in this day and age without their genetics being recorded somewhere. Even his employment—"

"I know," Joe said. "It would seem to indicate this will be an interesting problem. Perhaps too interesting."

But neither he nor I had any idea how interesting it would be. For the next week, we beat our heads against the impossibility of finding out who Narkissus Humel had been. Oh, we knew all about his employment in New Oxford, and Joe had read all his books and monographs.

He'd spent most of the week reading, in fact, while I did the boring work of searching for references to Narkissus Humel before his date of employment. There were none. There weren't even any references to his marriage to Idelle Zay, or whether he'd married someone else before her.

It was as though he were Athena, who'd sprang fully armed and adult from Zeus's head. Narkissus Humel had, seemingly, been born fully grown-up and in possession of a degree in criminal investigation and enough background experience and track record that he could be hired by New Oxford, and also married to a Galaxy-wide famous artist, Idelle Zay, and yet...

"It's completely impossible," I told Joe in frustration on the eighth day of turning over the dustiest corners of the Internet.

Joe sat at his desk, with his feet on the desktop—a bad habit of his I kept telling him would damage the tricomp built into the top—and his chair tilted back, reading one of Narkissus's books, *The Impossible Crime.* The title and cover materialized mid-air above the reader as Joe pressed the pause button. A boring cover, of a dagger floating in blue smoke. The sort of cover only academic presses use.

"Um?" he asked, looking up, his expression as bewildered as though I'd announced my head was made of cheese.

"This entire thing is completely impossible," I said. "There is no possible way that he could have been hired as a professor by New Oxford—*New Oxford*, Joe—with no record of his life prior to that moment."

Joe looked put upon, and I didn't take it personally. He never looked happy when anyone interrupted his reading. He tended to be completely into his material and paid no attention to the world around him. He resented it when the world didn't return the favor.

"There have been cases of great impostors," he said. "Haven't there? People who will turn up one day and become great medtechs, or lawyers, or news mediators, without ever having had training for it. And no one catches them, sometimes for years. Why shouldn't there be a great many who aren't ever caught? Perhaps that was Narkissus."

I shook my head. "It doesn't work that way," I said. "Not with New Oxford. He could have, I grant you, gotten a job that way at one of the lesser universities, perhaps one in some backwater world." He stared attentively at me, his face blank, and I felt like I had to explain further. "Look, it's like the training you took, that allows you to investigate anywhere in the Galaxy. The establishment you attended is the only one, and costs a small fortune. In the same way..." I paused. "Well, New Oxford prepares you for jobs that span the Galaxy, for licenses in medicine, or justice, or whatever, that are valid in every world in the Galaxy.

"It would have been easy for Narkissus to arrive at some place of no particular importance, say, Zegawa or Surary, and approached their local institute of criminology. Talk a good game, have a forged doctorate from... Well, most likely from New Oxford, pay someone in records to confirm he'd graduated there, and he would take chair the next day.

"They might never even check his genetic record, or make sure he really had graduated from New Oxford. Have a decent knowledge of the field, and they'd be happy enough to hire him."

Joe nodded minimally, but still looked blank. I didn't know if he was trying to understand what I had told him, or if he thought I made no sense.

"New Oxford hires by invitation," I said. "They look at publications, and have someone...well, someone like us investigate a potential hire. You won't even know you're under consideration, until they call you and offer you a position. So, if they hired Narkissus..."

"He had to have a record of publications, and work," he said. "Somewhere."

"Exactly," I said. "But there is nothing. And you don't marry someone like Idelle Zay without the news getting interested," I said. "She is well-known enough that there would be reports, and someone would wonder at it."

"But there isn't?" he said.

I shook my head.

Joe put his reader on the table facedown, something he rarely did when he hadn't finished reading whatever he'd started. I'd known him to read all night just to finish something. His reaction meant I had interested him. "But surely someone like Idelle Zay would have a record of having married him?" he asked. "Even if no news reported it?"

"That is the next problem," I said. "You see, Idelle Zay is one of those artists who disappear for long periods of time. Just drops out of sight. Yes, she was famous when she married him, but she disappeared from public view for about five years, and then came back with the work that made her famous. *Home.* And by the time there were reports on that work, she was married to Narkissus."

Joe frowned. Not at me. It was the peculiar frown he had when he was trying to figure something out. "Did you hire anyone else to follow up on either of their records, find out what they were doing?" he asked.

I shrugged. "No one of consequence. A couple of archive searchers, and I've called Jim a few times."

"So," Joe said. He leaned back and stared at the ceiling for a long time. "I suppose you couldn't get hold of Zay?"

"She is in one of her periods of disappearance." I cleared my throat. "I don't suppose anything you read by him told you anything I don't know or started any new line of enquiry?"

He shook his head. "Nothing but that Narkissus Humel was a very powerful intellect, the sort of man who could know—" He shrugged. "The sort of man who could pull off building a completely new life and erasing his past record, while retaining a professorship at New Oxford." He laughed a little, like he was making a joke. "You know what I mean."

"I suppose I do," I said. "I suppose we'll have to give up the case."

Joe looked like he'd swallowed a lemon.

"Uncle Gul said we could give up and keep the down payment."

"Sure, but if you reported that right, and I know you did, it would be permissible if we found it was too dangerous to continue. But this is not. It's more that we hit a wall. After a full week of investigation." He sighed and sat up, running his fingers back through his hair, in a gesture that denoted exasperation. "I suppose I'll have to call him. But you know, too many cases like this—"

I knew exactly what he meant. Too many cases like this, and we'd have to give up this field of endeavor, and his blue-sky dreaming of doing something else would become all too dire necessity. We'd have to figure out a way to make a living that didn't involve a reputation for solving impossible crimes or very complex puzzles.

"All right," I said.

Joe dialed the number Uncle Gul had given him. It rang through to New Oxford. And it rang a long time, before at last a hologram of Uncle Gul formed in the middle of the room.

It was the Uncle Gul—oh, sorry, the Gulbahar Felix the Galaxy knew, the jovial professor of history with the vast knowledge of every world and every period, who dressed like everyone's favorite uncle, in understated, slightly worn suits, and who blinked amicably at the tricam.

"Mr. Felix," Joe started.

But Uncle Gul blinked and smiled, and not in Joe's direction, and said, "Well, I am sorry not to be here. This is a recorded holo. Please leave your information, and I'll return—"

Joe turned off the holo, abruptly, and dialed someone else with a push of a button on his desk.

James Brighton formed in the middle of the room, almost immediately, behind his messy desk. I'd never understood why while everyone worked on holo and virtual files, Jim's desk must be cluttered with readers, data gems and piles and piles of objects that I suspected contained recordings and data. But it always looked like that. There were also several empty cups amid the objects, as there always were.

Jim also blinked without looking directly at us, and for a moment I thought we'd reached another pre-recorded message. But then he touched something on his desk and looked at Joe and then at myself. "I— You look like there is a problem?"

"Gulbahar Felix gave us a number for us to reach him at," Joe said. To those who didn't know him he might sound very upset, but I could tell he was utterly bewildered. "But he is not answering, and it occurred to me..."

"You didn't hear?" Jim asked. And to our bewildered expressions, "Don't you two ever listen to the news? Gulbahar Felix was found collapsed in his home early this morning. Some automated alarm sounded when his vital signs crashed. I guess he had subscribed to one of the services that track such things? Anyway, when they found him, they thought he had collapsed naturally. They now think he was injected with some kind of a poison, but they haven't managed to identify which."

"He is dead?" Joe asked.

"No. He is being kept alive in the life support unit of New Oxford's main hospital, but he is not conscious, or at least not coherent."

"And there are no suspects as to who did this?"

Jim shook his head. "No. There was an injector mark on his neck, but his door hadn't been forced in, and there was no indication of who might have been in. The house wasn't set to record visitors, and—" Jim sighed. "I never told you this, but a DNA examination of the scene discovered no DNA but Felix's. So, no one knows who visited, or what poison he was administered or why. All we know is that he was given poison. Law enforcement and investigators in New Oxford don't think it was self-administered, both because of the position of the injector mark, and because no one has found the injector, so it must have been taken out of the scene."

We talked with Jim a few more minutes, but nothing else of importance was said. In the end, it was obvious that whatever had happened, it belonged to the same category of inexplicable as what might have happened to Narkissus's records before his being hired by New Oxford.

"You realize," Joe said, as he hung up on Jim. His face was set in grim lines. "That there is only one thing we can do."

"Nothing, until or unless Uncle Gul wakes up?" I said.

He half-opened his mouth in shock. "No," he said. "We have to go to Elysium."

Elysium

Elysium was all it had been advertised. We had to journey there in two jumps, one to orbit in Far Itravine. From space Far Itravine looked just like a water planet, shining and blue. I'm told Earth looks much the same, but the only time I'd been there I was five or six, and I didn't remember much of anything, save the white balcony and worn tiles of a hotel that Daddy was considering buying.

From there we jumped to Elysium. It must have had a similar amount of water, because I understand—though I never studied interplanetary geology or ecology—all Earth-like planets have a lot of water, but perhaps because of where we emerged in orbit, the world looked like a luscious green and blue jewel, with the green winding, snake-like from top to bottom, a shining spiral embracing the blue. Emerald upon sapphire.

Closer in, we could tell that the green was a succession of islands, each of them seeming to have a distinctive style of architecture, and a way in which it was designed. Even from space this was obvious, though I can't exactly explain how. It was a bit like being in orbit around an amusement park. It had that feel of being over-manicured, too clean. And each region shining with a particular tone of green.

We'd investigated the planet before we approached, and had decided we'd land on an island on the periphery, not near the largest islands where the two cities—probably fully-planned, designed cities—that graced this world were located.

One of the things we'd found about Elysium was that it was not entirely devoted to institutions catering to the elderly, as we'd been led to believe by Uncle Gul's cursory description.

While the planet was indeed all owned by a consortium that cared for the elderly, it was possible for those over a hundred years—the planet would let no one under one hundred live there—to rent one of the many private homes, or even one of the private islands, entire.

Some people retired to Elysium, it seemed, not because they saw the end of life approaching, but because it was a relatively cheap place to enjoy your retirement years. In fact, as we entered the atmosphere and flew over the world, it became obvious that it was a leisure world, the oceans littered with flotillas of pleasure vessels, colorful sails hoisted between glittering sea and shining sun. The beaches were filled with people. And there was a sound from the world, of busy people living a busy life.

After we landed, on one of the far-off islands where mostly supply ships landed, Joe said, "It's not all like that, you know. In the central islands, I understand most of the places are assisted living of some sort, from those who need help with the business of daily living, to those who need nanites and machines to keep them alive. And there is an island devoted completely to the ashes of those who were cremated. It's a garden." He looked upset, somehow. "There are also underground chambers, where those who choose to do so have their bodies preserved in ice, or time-stasis, which I suppose makes as much sense as anything else. I must tell you," he said. "That I find all of this very depressing and more than a little disturbing: to isolate yourself to a place that is populated exclusively by people who are very old and expect to die soon. It seems like... Like going somewhere and hoping Death pays a visit." He shuddered.

"I expect you wouldn't want us to do that when we're over one hundred, then?" I asked playfully. We'd married for life, instead of the normal fifty-year term, and I wasn't even sure why except at the time, it seemed like a good way of spiting Daddy. But honestly, most marriages didn't last past the fifty-year mark, if they lasted that long. People changed too much in the course of half a century for it to make any sense to stay married anymore. And while I didn't often engage in thinking that far, and didn't like the idea that there would be a time when Joe and I weren't married anymore, it was folly to imagine we'd still be together seventy-five years in the future when I turned a hundred, or even sixty-five years in the future, when he did.

He didn't say any of that, or even acknowledge my attempt at a joke. Instead, he said, "Not if I'm in my senses, no."

He sighed. "Anyway, this port is much cheaper, which means our ship will call a lot less attention. I have filed papers saying I intend to visit my aunt Valli Arana."

"Is there anyone by that name on Elysium?" I asked.

He grinned. "Yes. And she is even my aunt. She was my grandmother's sister. I haven't had much contact with her, but when I searched the records for someone I was related to as an excuse for coming to Elysium, I was very glad to find her name. It makes our visit completely legitimate and completely unrelated to the Narkissus matter. Not that anyone should connect us to the Narkissus matter, since the only person who knows we are on the case is Jim."

"Who never talks to the public at large unless he's paid to."

"True. But I don't know how well Gulbahar Felix covered his tracks when he came to visit us, and there was undeniably someone who recommended me to him. Now, I'm sure if he'd been obvious someone would have contacted us by now, to figure out what his business with us was. On the other hand, it's possible that they think he visited us about something quite different. In fact, it's possible the attack on him had a reason completely unrelated to Narkissus. You know the usual reasons."

"Sure, money, or guilty knowledge of sexual jealousy." Though I had a great deal of trouble connecting Uncle Gul with sexual jealousy in any direction, either of him, or of his being jealous of someone.

"Right. It's quite possible whoever decided to take him out did so for reasons having absolutely nothing to do with us, or with his seeing us."

"But?" I said, asking for the completion of the thought I could feel hanging mid-air.

"But that is not the way I'd bet, and so I thought it was a good idea to disguise the whole thing under the appearance of visiting Auntie Arana."

The place where we landed wasn't precisely squalid. On a scale of slum to...well, Daddy's private docking pad, it was about halfway up. For a spaceport, it had the usual amenities of a docking station used mostly by freighters and commercial liners transporting workers: three restaurants, a lot of shops with moderately priced merchandise, including alcohol and sweets, and an extensive complex of shops devoted to mechanical parts and other such things that might be needed by people repairing ships.

I spent the day browsing all these shops and reconnoitering the terrain, while Joe ostensibly visited his aunt.

He'd come back pensive and worried. I'd made us dinner, programming the cooker with one of Joe's recipes—I'd known near nothing about cooking when we'd first married, but he liked creating recipes, even for our limited cooker—but he'd talked little. Mostly, strangely, about Aunt Arana.

I will forever remember his looking past my shoulder, as though he were staring into the infinite—and not the brushed-steel bulkhead behind my head—and saying, "I wonder if the long lives we have now are a blessing. I mean, you know, I wouldn't want to be like ancient people, like people in the time of Nick Rhodes, for instance, old at sixty and dead at eighty. I like the idea that I'll still be around at a hundred. Maybe that we—" He looked at me for the briefest of moments, and then alone, and I knew both what he wanted to say, and why he didn't say it. He wanted to say, "Maybe that we'll still be together," and what held him back was not his uncertainty that he wanted this, but his fear I wouldn't want it. That the rich girl would be tired of playing working-class games.

To be fair, social class difference or not, very few marriages lasted more than fifty years, and most people went through three or—for the exceptionally long-lived—four in their lives. And perhaps it was foolish of me to think we'd be the exception, that we'd stay married like the people of old, till death do us part, each a bulwark and defense against the wide Galaxy for the other.

And I said nothing, because it would be like admitting that he was right, that there were similar thoughts in my head.

Instead, I reached across the table and touched his hand. He smiled, the briefest of smiles, and then said, "It's just, I think Aunt Arana, inside, you know, and in talks with me... It's like she's still twenty. But she can't move or do much. It's like she's a prisoner in her own body."

I blinked. I'd heard this before. Some friends of Daddy's thought that we should "humanely" kill all the old people, all handicapped people, perhaps even poor people. So, they wouldn't be a burden on society. "Well," I said. "Did she tell you she wants to die?"

He looked surprised. "Oh, no. No. And I don't mean that. I wouldn't want her to have died, Lilly. She is one— Well..." He paused, as though considering what to say, and his next words told me why. Joe didn't willingly talk about his parents. I never understood why, and I wasn't sure what had happened in his childhood. But I wasn't even absolutely sure where Joe had been born. Sometimes, things he said gave me the impression he had been born on Earth, Mother Terra itself. "Well," he said again. "You know, or perhaps not, that I didn't have much in common with my parents, but Aunt Arana and I...we're symps. We connect. She was a detective when she was much younger. She must have been atomic fire and interstellar drive. She told me stories—" He sighed. "I just wish we could solve aging. That we could make people be young for the duration of their natural lives."

I got up, got our used plates, disposed of them. Over coffee, I told him, "You know, humans have wanted that since ever. We've tried to get eternal youth since long before we left Terra behind."

"Right," he said. "Nick Rhodes and the Peaches of Immortality. When the Chinese Emperor hires Nick to find them."

I grinned at him. I didn't know and will never know if it was stupid or endearing that my very intelligent husband got all his cultural and historical references from a mersi series. I was glad it was a series largely acknowledged to be accurate, though at a distance of ten thousand years, who knew? I supposed some centuries ran together.

Later, after we'd put away dishes, Joe had called up the music player on the squawker, and played a tango.

This was how we met. He'd crossed the club where I was with my friends, to ask me to dance with him. And in his arms, I'd found a certainty, an acceptance I'd never known. As though we were two long-separated halves of the same whole.

That night, I leaned into Joe, following the music by instinct, feeling my husband's body warm and supporting leading me.

When I woke up, Joe was gone. There was a note delivered to me when I turned on the desk comp. Joe's voice said, "Hey, Lilly. I woke up with an idea, and I'm going to chase it. I should be back in a couple of hours."

Because he'd said he'd be back soon, I didn't leave the ship, but instead stayed at my desk, and got on with collating and filing some of our older cases. Joe got too bored by this work to do it.

I hadn't worried about Joe's continued absence until six hours had passed. And even then, I wasn't terribly concerned. Joe sometimes met unexpected wrinkles in a case and pursued it with monomania until it cracked. I'd eaten alone. And eventually I'd gone to bed, sleeping the kind of half-sleep one does when expecting someone. But Joe hadn't come back.

I shuddered at the thought he might have come back now.

There was something to the movements of the borg, something to the look—

I looked at the borg with his feet on my desk, and ran through what I could do. And what I couldn't.

I sent a panic code from my portable com. Joe had programmed it when we were first married. If I sent the highest panic code—this one—Joe would come back. He would come back right away by any means necessary, no matter what he had been doing, no matter who tried to stand in his way. Before that, he would com back, and ask me what was wrong.

I waited, holding my breath, looking at the borg sitting at Joe's desk, the borg who thought he was Nick Rhodes, and I prayed. Which was difficult, because I hadn't been raised to believe in any religion. Joe believed in God, though he'd never discussed details with me. He wore a little golden cross on a chain around his neck. He'd told me it was a religious thing, though it wasn't any of the symbols I knew. But since I didn't know where Joe came from, maybe it was a local planetary religion.

Right then I concentrated on that image, of that cross, and pointed out, reasonably, to the divinity it symbolized that since Joe was one of his devotees, he might want to do whatever was needed to ensure that Joe was alive and hadn't been borged. And that he came back to me.

No answer came. From Joe's com, or from whatever divinity might be listening in.

So. Let's assume that Joe had been borged. If he hadn't, he was in trouble bad, anyway. But if he had—

If he had, the brain in this borg was all that remained of Joe. And by law, by the law of all human worlds, interplanetarily enforced, I was supposed to call the authorities and tell them there was a borg here, and they were supposed to come and destroy it.

Destroy all that was left of Joe.

And The Rock Cried Out

I'd never had to make decisions involving our cases or our lives. For a moment, hysterically, I thought that all I was trained to do was dance and look good in hologram pictures of the rich and famous.

But damn it, I'd chosen this life myself. I'd chosen to marry Joe. Yes, I loved him, but perhaps I also didn't love my comfy, cozy, confined life. Perhaps it was all of that.

I realized that I had clenched my hands hard on my suit.

What should I do? What was logical to do in these circumstances?

Well, I could leave the ship, go to Aunt Arana, find out if she'd seen Joe. I could trace his movements, and perhaps find him, tied up or locked up. That was logical, wasn't it?

Perfectly logical. Only not quite right.

To do so, I'd have to go, leaving this borg in the ship. A borg who thought he was Nick Rhodes, and who would probably pilot the ship somewhere, leaving me stranded in Elysium. Or I could call in and say there was a borg, and watch them destroy it and perhaps lose all that remained of Joe.

No. Not acceptable.

Right. Think. Calm. I put my fingers on my brow and tried to breathe in measured, controlled breaths. I had to think. Joe said that Nick Rhodes always said that panic can kill. I would not panic. Both our lives might depend on it.

Let's suppose that this borg wasn't Joe. If he wasn't Joe, why had he come straight to my ship, trying to get in, and obviously remembering the code?

The only reason for that if he weren't Joe was that someone was setting us up. There would be a group of people following the borg, and they would denounce us for keeping a borg and not calling the authorities.

I tried tentatively, "Er... Why did you come here?"

The banked blue fires in the artificial eyes glowed brighter, and he looked in my direction. "Why, Stella, I always come home to you."

Right, and if he said that to investigators, they'd probably decide that Joe and I had somehow borged this person and kept him in the ship. Which means—they'd kill us both.

And if Joe were the borg?

Well, it would explain why he had come here and knew the code, and why all his gestures were familiar. What it wouldn't explain was why a borg, less than twenty-four hours made, had recovered enough consciousness to escape his captors and come barreling home.

Which meant the overwhelming chance was, still, that someone or something had allowed him to escape and come here.

And that meant the gambit was the same. If someone had sent the borg to our ship, no matter who the borg was, it was an attempt to silence us permanently.

Which made it imperative that I—

That I get out of here as soon as possible.

Before I'd finished the thought, I was in the navigation room, and pulling up the various maps that would take me to various places.

You see, I don't know how to program interstellars. I'm not Uncle Gul. At best I could use pre-programmed courses and get somewhere. And Joe had made sure I had some pre-programmed courses in the system that would allow me to get to places where I could find help: Elfenheim. New Oxford. Far Itravine, where Joe had some friends.

I'd picked New Oxford, where I could get help from Jim, and was about to push the "Start" button on the routine execution, when a voice crackled over the com:

Attention, West 35th Street*: for reasons of world security, we're putting an interdiction on your movements. Officials will be aboard momentarily. Do not offer resistance.*

I screamed. Fortunately, without using the com. I'm not sure what my incoherent scream of rage in response would have done, but I suspected that it would have gotten us shot out of the sky immediately.

"Stella." The borg stood at the door to the navigation room, his huge bulk casting a shadow on the controls.

I don't know what I answered. Part of me was terrified of the large thing in the doorway, while the other part of my mind was frantically running through everything and everyone I had ever loved, sure that I was about to be disintegrated into atoms within seconds.

The borg stepped in and nudged me away from the controls and pushed buttons. I didn't know what he was pushing. I think I closed my eyes. If you're going to die, anyway, does it matter if you die by translating your ship into impossible coordinates, or simply being vaporized by some kind of anti-ship cannon?

I don't know how long his reprogramming took, but it must have been near-instant.

I felt the kick as the ship climbed to orbit, and the weird stomach-turning-inside-out of transition. In between there was a gentle rocking of the ship that meant—I think—that we'd been shot at, but the shot missed.

And then there was nothing. I opened my eyes. The borg had turned to me. The lights in his eyes burned lambent-blue and the voice that came out was Joe's. "Lilly," he said. The lights went out, with an effect of blinking. "We're... I brought us nowhere. I think we're safe here." And then, in that other voice, the Nick Rhodes voice, "I will go to the office now, Stella. We should consult about the case."

I nodded to him. My mouth was dry. I wanted to cry. I was now sure, whatever else was true, that there was a fragment of my husband in this creature. Whether it was physical or programming, I didn't know. But whatever it was, it was breaking my heart. I wanted Joe. I wanted Joe, my husband. I didn't want—

And then I processed *I brought us nowhere.*

I got on the controls, looked at the coordinates. Nowhere. Nowhere was accurate. The only question was, why? Whatever the creature was, whatever he had done, why bring us nowhere?

Did it make any sense? In that space between what was or had been Joe and whatever was going on in this fresh-made borg, why had he brought us nowhere?

I didn't know what I had told him, but something to my clenched stomach, my clenched fists told me it wasn't all irrational, not just impulses. That there was some reasoning behind the decision.

This borg—let's assume for the moment he was Joe—hadn't been irrational. Joe wasn't irrational, so it made perfect sense that a borg with his brain wouldn't be.

Being convinced he was Nick Rhodes wasn't actually irrational. It was strange, bizarre, but it might be the most functional illusion possible to help cope with the moment.

The problem of being nowhere, of course, was that we'd have to get out of nowhere.

And allow me to explain, as well as I can, because as I've explained, I am no interstellar pilot, and certainly no astrophysicist, so I don't know the proper words or formulae: we weren't *nowhere*. Not really. We couldn't be nowhere. We were in *what was called in pilot-lingo nowhere*. Which, if I understood the pilots and retired pilots who attended evenings at my father's house, was...an unregistered location, unmapped, and not set up for transition to other node points.

The schrodingers—I think the real name of the tech was *probability ships*, but they'd been called schrodingers since the mid-twenty-first century, when they were invented—could theoretically translate along any set of coordinates, point to point, instantaneously. Their nickname was the result of the first ships built not taking time into account, and therefore sending ships ten thousand years into the past, or presumably the future. Or—as far as their creators knew—making one-third of the ships simply disappear.

When they'd figured out the problem, for a while—until the discovery of Kyre tech—they'd used the stabilizing influence of a mind-linked human to make sure they translated into the present time only. By that time there had been human colonies seeded and lost, on purpose or accidentally, all over the universe. Most of the human worlds started with a lost schrodinger. Not that they all admitted it. Having been in worlds for ten thousand years or more, many believed they were indigenous, and some refused to revise their beliefs when contacted by the rest of the human race.

In the present day, schrodingers could work by computer alone. But unless you were a skilled pilot, you'd send it to one of the mapped and programmed nodes, from which you could translate to another mapped and programmed node. Which is why I'd tried to translate to orbit around New Oxford. Which had been doable from the programmed node orbit of Elysium. From here...

I stared at the display which gave only coordinates. Well, from here, it was going to be hard. The good news, though, was that we were also, probably, untraceable and unfindable by normal means. Unless someone with a lot of tech knowledge sent for us.

Because I was myself, I looked at the reserves in the ship. But that was all right. We'd taken in water and air at Elysium, upon landing, so our recycling systems, which

I engaged, would keep us going for three months. Six if I used the extreme recycling the ship could do. It wasn't exactly healthy, but it would keep me alive.

The problem, of course, was that being far from everything I couldn't really investigate, could I?

Then again, how could I investigate? I was not trained for anything except typing, accounting, dancing and looking pretty. And arguably I wasn't trained in the first two. I'd just picked them up, along the line.

Right. I'd find out why the borg had done what he had done.

I walked into the office, feeling as though I were keeping my inner turmoil under a rigid envelope of control. I couldn't allow myself to think this was Joe: all that I had left of Joe. I couldn't allow myself to wonder if there was a way to get my husband back, or if I was in fact a widow. And I definitely couldn't allow myself to wonder if I should call the borg in and have it put out of its misery. I could say it had kidnapped me. I could say—

I realized I was walking with the sort of gait and posture that I'd used as a young girl, when my father required me to appear at a party with people who made me uncomfortable.

There are advantages to the type of upbringing I had. They're not what I would wish on anyone else, but they are what they are. And one of them is the ability to present a serene front, an almost haughty demeanor, even if you're falling apart internally.

I sat behind my desk. The borg was at Joe's desk, feet resting on it, chair tilted back, in a position that was so much like Joe that tears prickled behind my eyes. But I wouldn't allow them to actually materialize.

Instead I asked, in my polite-social voice, "Why did you take us nowhere?"

The borg straightened. The chair creaked. *We need to have the chair replaced,* I thought. And then I thought that was stupid. I couldn't go on living with the borg, even if he were Joe. I couldn't. It wasn't sane.

The flickering blue lights of his eyes turned to me. The features moved, imperceptibly, to be an almost-smile. "Isn't it obvious?" he asked.

At least the voice was Nick Rhodes, because the words were so much Joe, that if the voice had matched them, I might have come undone.

"Not to me," I said.

The smile became a grin, even though the features weren't that mobile, and the material that made them couldn't allow them to be. I guess there was very little mobility needed to give the artificial faces of borgs the impression of being human. Although why they should have expressions at all I didn't know. "Well, that's because you're not thinking, Stella. You believe they planted..." I got the impression he was wildly searching for vocabulary, which had to be lacking when he was in Nick Rhodes's mind. After all, borgs hadn't existed in the early twentieth. At least I didn't think so. I wasn't a history buff, and I knew that period dramas weren't always accurate. I guessed I'd have to study— No. I was not going to continue living with a borg, even if it was all that remained of my husband.

"Well, Stella," he resumed, and folded his hands on his chest as he spoke. "If they planted forbidden tech on you, and intended to denounce you for it, obviously they were calling out a wanted bulletin at the same time. If we went anywhere but nowhere, then we would be destroyed."

"That's all very well," I said. "But how am I supposed to do any investigation and find out who set us up?" If I remembered correctly, from all of Joe's enthusing about it, Stella actually did all the *legwork,* as I think they called it. That is, the actual, physical investigation involved in their cases. Nick couldn't show his face—or wouldn't show his face. Because of his disfigurement in the First World War, he wore a ceramic mask over his face. And for some reason he thought this would upset people enough that it was best for Stella to investigate.

I remembered Joe saying the suspension of disbelief required was for Stella being able to do investigation and fight, since at the time women weren't taken seriously, and also, of course, without nano enhancements, their strength couldn't match that of males.

The borg stared at the ceiling, and for a moment I thought he was being smug; then I realized he was just doing what Joe did when he was thinking.

I would not cry.

"I can set up the console, so you can remote-call anyone you wish, without giving our location away," he offered. "Though perhaps it is a case of figuring out who to call? Whom can you call that you can trust completely? Is this a case of 'And The Rock Cried Out'?"

"The rock what?"

"It's an old religious song," the borg said. "'There's no hiding place down here/There's no hiding place down here/Well, I run to the rock just to hide my face/And the rocks cried out, no hiding place/There's no hiding place down here.'"

"Charming," I said. Even as my brain processed that if there was a borging—of just harboring a borg—charge against me, I might very well be out of hiding places. Except for maybe the Qan Empire, there was no safe place for a borger. And the Qan Empire wasn't safe for anyone.

The borg made a sound that might have been sudden, startled laugh when processed by whatever he used for vocal cords. "I often felt that way in the trenches, at the front, under the cannonade. Surrounded by dead men. Water in the trench, tainted with rot. And the slightest movement above the trench, the lighting of a cigarette, could get you killed. Nowhere to hide."

I didn't say anything. Joe had never been at the front, certainly not in World War One, Earth's first global war. And neither had this deranged machine-human hybrid.

The question was, was there a rock that would hide me? Metaphorically speaking?

Casting the Dice

In the end, I called Jim. Perhaps I'd always been going to. The borg set up the controls, and I trusted they were now secure.

Once I got Jim, I knew they were, because he'd had no idea who was calling. Hence the surprise when he saw me.

Surprise and relief. "Lilly," he said. He sat behind his desk, with its permanent clutter, and leaned back on the chair, all boneless. "Are you all right? Is Joe all right? I answered this and set it up to secret, on the off-chance— You wouldn't believe what I heard over the news channels."

I couldn't keep the tears back then. They most inconveniently poured out, though I tried not to let them affect my voice or demeanor, as I told Jim what had happened. I didn't want Jim to get involved in this or come to my defense because he had to. I wanted—

I wanted him to know what the stakes were. Because by pulling him into this adventure, I was making him, too, an accomplice in borging, and potentially on the wanted list of every civilized or would-be civilized government in the world.

So, I tried to keep my voice dispassionate, and to tell him everything in the most un-emotional way possible. It wasn't easy. And I wasn't entirely successful, or perhaps Jim was more susceptible to female tears than I'd thought. His face looked more and more anguished while I talked.

As I finished, and sat there, on the chair in the pilot cabin, as I'd refused to call from the office—I didn't know how the borg would react if he heard my narration—and closed the door to the cabin, he was silent. Tears kept falling down my face, some biological process I wasn't sure I could control. It didn't matter what my mind was doing; the water would trickle out. And Jim sat behind his desk, face ashen-white and anguished.

At last, he ran his hand back through his hair, and said, "Devil's coil."

Or at least I think that's what he said.

He took an audible gulp of air, and another, and then he said, "Lilly, what are your plans? What do you need from me?"

I shrugged. "I don't know. I don't want to—I can't go on living with a borg, of course."

"No." Jim hesitated. "You could claim it kidnapped you. The fact that it took you nowhere, something you don't know how to do, should speak to the veracity—"

"No." I realized it had been a yell as Jim flinched, and said, more calmly, "No. That's not what I meant. I mean, I don't want to live with a borg, but if it is Joe—"

Jim nodded, and said nothing. His face, even its overgrown stubble, looked like it had been cast in glassteel, immobile.

"I haven't decided on that," I said. And tried to pretend the decision wasn't potentially killing all that remained of my husband. "But more importantly, I don't know how to investigate the case Joe was following up on. I don't know how to find out who— Whom he was pursuing, and who is responsible for either borging Joe, or setting us up as borging accomplices, so we'll be killed. And I don't know how to do it while staying hidden, so whoever is after us doesn't kill me." A giggle that I didn't see coming escaped me. "And I have no idea if you want to get involved in all this."

Jim shook his head. "I never told you where I came from, did I, back in college?" And before I could respond to the non-sequitur, he said, "Ufraglio."

He said it as though it should mean something to me, and at what must have been my utterly blank look—did he mistake me for a geographer?—he laughed, a startled laugh. "You really have no idea, do you? I come from Egraina, the capital city of Ufraglio. It wasn't easy getting a scholarship when the main industry of my world of origin is... Leverage. Interplanetary criminal organizations, blackmail, and other lovely cultural habits." His widening smile showed his teeth in what might have been almost a growl. "Though of course, perhaps that was considered a plus, since what I wanted to do was news aggregation, an industry where most people aren't exactly clean."

I processed what he'd said. Interplanetary criminal organizations were everywhere, really, and from what I understood from conversations at Daddy's, they were always at least influenced by people with money. But that didn't mean anything in the context of our conversation. Was Jim offering me covert criminal influence, or what?

"No, you have no idea. Let me explain. When most people you know operate outside the law, and when your family is beholden to people who operate outside the law, as my family was, because frankly in the capital city there is no other way of earning money, you learn to work within it. The fragility of your position, of the position of everyone around you is such that should anyone talk, everyone will be destroyed. There is an ancient proverb that says there is no honor among thieves.

"It must have been contrived by someone who was very law-abiding. There *is* honor among thieves. There must be, because when you're operating outside the law, that's the only thing that keeps you from falling through and being destroyed."

"I still don't understand what this means in the context of asking you for help in something that might get you killed."

He shrugged. "Only this: without yours and Joe's help in...that situation, my only way out might have been suicide. So, I owe you my life. And therefore, according to the honor code in which I was brought up, I don't really have a choice. It's a life for a life, isn't it? I'm ready to help you in whatever you need. Just tell me what you need."

I first checked on the condition of Uncle Gul. It was unchanged. I asked him if he'd tracked down Narkissus Humel, or anything relating to him. He said he was close to maybe tracking down Idelle Zay. A local exhibit house in New Oxford was expecting a piece from her any day. And Jim was sure he could track her from that. Perhaps she had some insight into Narkissus.

"But of course," he said. "That won't tell you what is going on in Elysium. Nor what happened to Joe. I mean, it's possible the borg has been mentally conditioned to react like Joe—including the obsession with Nick Rhodes—and that the real Joe is somewhere in Elysium, besieged or in trouble."

"I know," I said. And then, "I must go rescue him if that's the case. And if it's not— If it's not, I must find out who borged him, and...and bring the culprit to justice."

"Um," Jim said. He didn't say anything else. He didn't need to say anything else. I was more aware than anyone else might be of my lack of training, and my inadequate experience in investigations.

"I know. Whoever it was, they still got to Joe some way or another. And Joe was...is very good at his job, but hear me out: if Joe is hiding, I'm the only one who can get him out of hiding and get him to talk to me."

Jim opened his mouth, then closed it. He nodded once. "But you can't go to Elysium under your own appearance, or name," he said. "So how would Joe know it was you, and know to come out?"

I tilted my head. "I have an idea," I said. "But it will take some research. Meanwhile..."

"Meanwhile?"

"How do I get out of here? And what can we do about the borg until I am done?"

"You should turn the borg in. It can be done through intermediaries, so it's not traceable to you, and then they will be unable to pin a capital case on you when—"

"No," I said. "I haven't made a decision. You can't make that decision for me."

Jim looked at me a long time, then pursed his lips. But he didn't tell me I was out of my mind, though I obviously was. Instead, he said, "If you want to keep the borg alive, over time, you're going to need to purchase some highly-regulated and difficult-to-find compounds. I'm not saying it's impossible for you to do that without being suspected of borging, but I'm saying it will be difficult."

"Why?" I asked. "Not why will it be difficult, but why do I need to purchase those? I thought borgs—"

He shook his head. "They neither eat nor excrete," Jim reminded me. "And while they get their energy from Kyre batteries, the fluid that, in the place of blood, keeps the brain and spinal cord alive and fed still needs replacing and cleaning."

"Oh," I said. "How long—"

"I can investigate, but I think you have a couple of weeks."

"So, I'll have to decide in two weeks."

"At most."

"Then it would be good if I get started. Where can I port the ship that will be safe? And how do I do it?"

"I don't think you can." He sounded brutally final. "Not with that ship, with the registrations it has." He pursed his lips again. "Give me your coordinates."

I did, and he nodded, as he entered them into some device. "I can be there in twenty-four standard hours, to retrieve you. Can you be ready?"

"Uh, and the borg?"

"I propose we leave it aboard ship," Jim said. "After explaining to it that death for all of us is the result of it doing something unexpected. I think from what you said that it is rational enough to wait. I'll bring a...ah... Unregistered interstellar I have access to, and take you wherever you wish to go. We'll figure out a way to disguise you, though I still don't know how you expect Joe to see through the disguise. If he's hiding."

"Leave that to me," I said. "See you in twenty-four hours."

I turned the com off, and sat for a few minutes. It was entirely possible, given the nature of the situation I found myself in, that Jim planned to betray me. It was entirely possible, not to say probable, that he meant to come in with the law, and have me and the borg, whoever he was, destroyed. Some would say it was the rational thing for him—or anyone else—to do.

But I didn't think so. Granted, I had nothing more than our knowledge of Jim to go on. But what else could I go on? And who else could help me in this situation?

Arguably, Daddy might, and he had enough power and connections to protect me from about anything, including a borging charge. But if Joe was in Elysium and needed help, I wouldn't put it past Daddy to have Joe indicted of borging just to get me back. No. Perhaps that was too far. Possessive as my father was, he'd never been utterly ruthless without cause. But he might very well make our divorce a condition of rescuing Joe. And after that, he might make very sure that Joe could never come near me. There were things he could manipulate, for that result. And if the borg was Joe, Daddy would have him destroyed. There was no doubt of that.

Perhaps I would have the borg destroyed, too. Maybe. Perhaps I should.

I played with the wedding ring on my finger, the plain wedding band engraved with Joseph Aster on the inside. Perhaps I should. But that didn't mean I would.

And I wasn't going to let Daddy decide that for me.

No, the dice had been cast. And all I could do was hope that Jim played fairly.

Meanwhile I had to follow up on my idea, if Joe were stranded and hiding in Elysium, on how to signal to my husband that I was there to rescue him, while not being immediately obvious to anyone else.

I had an idea, but it needed investigating. Which required me to do something I'd never done before.

West 35th Street

It was raining in ancient New York City.

Well, no. Not the real New York City, but the New York City of the Nick Rhodes mersi series.

From what Joe had told me, it rained a lot, in almost all the episodes.

I'd no idea if rain was that normal in New York City in the late 1920s of Earth's Current Era. Or if in fact the city looked anything at all like it looked in this mersi representation.

I'd entered the mersi unit in the spare room. At the time, we had the cheapest possible mersi unit, which looked somewhat like one of the clamshell, ambient-control beds you get in the cheapest public dormitories. It is like that, too, in that while you're in there, and the top closed, it keeps your vital signs optimal: meaning it provides optimal temperature and oxygenation and everything else to keep your body alive, while your mind is experiencing adventures. I understand—though I've never had need of such a thing—the most expensive and specialized units, those used for geriatrics with significant health problems, will be ready to inject various medicines should your chosen adventure prove too exciting for your heart, for instance.

As I said, ours was a basic unit, a blue clamshell, looking somewhat like a cheap coffin, except coffins were rarely hooked up to various electronic units. Those looked cheap, too. They *were* cheap. Joe said the most affordable units did all the things the expensive—non-medically-specialized—units did, and he preferred to save his money for the purchase of mersi adventures. Most of all, he spent a lot of money for the top-of-the-line Nick Rhodes releases.

The top-of-the-line release was customizable. Not fully, of course. You couldn't rewrite the plot of episodes or change the essential adventure that you stepped into. The mysteries would be presented as the writers intended; the environment was as the writers created it. There might be some flexibility in plot, insofar as your decisions might alter how you achieved the solution, and sometimes there were more than one possible plots, and a randomizer made it possible to live through the adventure hundreds of times without getting the same solution twice.

Nick Rhodes Mersis were famous for this, in fact, and there were entire fan sites devoted to defending one plot and one solution over the hundreds of possible others.

But the difference between the basic edition and the top-of-the-line one was somewhat different: you were allowed to encode yourself, your personality, the way you acted and behaved as Nick Rhodes or Stella, or one of the other recurring characters, like Nick's Army-buddy and journalist friend Alex Finley. In the same way you could encode other looks and personality into all of those, other than the one you chose to play.

Because of the borg's insistence on calling me Stella, whether or not he'd been created with the use of Joe's brain, I had a suspicion I knew Joe had encoded not only himself, but also me, as Stella.

I only knew the half of it. My confirmation that he'd indeed encoded me as Stella, which by the way, would entail allowing the AI engine of the game to study trid recordings of me in various situations—not exactly a violation of privacy, since this mersi was only encoded for use in this unit and by one of its owners, that is, Joe or myself—came when I first closed the lid. The mersi unit identified me—since we owned it jointly, it was gen-coded to both of us—and immediately said, "Mersi user identified as Stella in Nick Rhodes serial. Do you wish to play this character? Yes/No?"

I could have quit right then. Maybe. I should add the other thing the mersi allows every user to do—not just the high-end user—is to play sequences that don't add to a change in plot. Extraneous sequences. Fans like Joe called them "day in the life."

You could go to Nick Rhodes's New York City and walk around; have a ham sandwich and a glass of milk at Stella's favorite deli; or stay in the house, between cases, and discuss religion, politics or history with Nick, cook with Loup Armel, whose life Nick had saved in an occupied village and who had followed Nick home to become his cook; you could go up on the top floor of the house where Ruedi Messer kept the rare volumes that were Nick's obsession.

All of this you could do without changing the plot or in any way affecting any of the stories. And Nick had told me that it was also possible, if not strictly legal, for a fan to encode the mersis with something that could be experienced by another fan.

In fan groups they traded the hack codes, and the way to do this, and some groups traded fan off-game experiences from romantic plots—and I presume sex—involving Stella or Nick, to silly moments in which, say, a random fan could go into his mersi and experience a birthday party thrown for him or her by Nick or his staff.

I understood that the Global War One Company, which had struck gold with Nick Rhodes after years of doing only middling-successful war games set in the twentieth century, stomped pretty hard on the more perverse or stranger of the fan creations and pretended not to know the rest.

It was good that I'd spent months listening to Joe telling me, excitedly, about this world in a fandom I didn't precisely participate in.

It was good, because it prepared me for the next announcement for the mersi: "Do you wish to play encoded emergency sequence one, created by Joe Aster in case his wife finds herself alone and in trouble?"

I didn't expect it to hit me so hard. Lying there, in that clamshell, which had absorbed the smell of Joe—his natural smell, his aftershave, the myriad unconscious notes that added up to "Joe" in my mind—and hearing that question made me realize that he'd thought of— Well, if not of everything, of a lot of things.

I almost started crying, and my hand shook so hard, I had trouble pushing the "Y" choice.

And then...

I suppose I should say it was like falling asleep. That's what people normally say, and how they describe a mersi experience, and I'd had that in commercial mersis, too. Perhaps it's a sequence that mersi designers put in.

In this one, I closed my eyes, and I was walking on the streets of old New York City, or as close to them as the designers could take me and the archeologists could decipher. Only, I presume, making it look better.

And I have to tell you that right here, in this sequence, I'm going to tell you the story as if you—yourself—have played the Nick Rhodes Mersis.

First, because so many people have played them. But second, because if I start explaining everything I mention, to bridge the gap between our time and Earth's end of the second millennium, people who have played the mersi or any mersi of that time are going to be bored to tears. Those who have never played it are going to be so fascinated with the descriptions they'll lose track of what I'm telling.

One of the attractions of the mersis over books—which Joe also loved—or vids and holos is that all that knowledge was right there in your head.

Walking the New York City streets, I didn't have to have it explained to me what sidewalks were, what crossing lights were; that the vehicles driving by in a glimmer of chrome and a smell of burned propellant were land-automobiles and burned gasoline.

Going into a mersi, you know anything that the person who would live in that environment would know. I understand that it's used by various diplomatic corps, artist academies, and explorer groups to teach skills because of this: because some of that back-brain knowledge lingers, even when you come out of the mersi.

The bad side, of course, is that you learn only as much as the mersi programmers knew: so, for serious study it is advised you also use books, holos and the lectures of people like Uncle Gul.

At any rate, I was walking the streets of New York City in the early twentieth century, as the sun set. I wore a tight, grey knee-length skirt, a matching coat—over a white blouse—and held an umbrella over my head.

The umbrella was because it was drizzling. Everything around me, from the cement sidewalks to the yellow taxis to the light poles, was wet, and glistened with a golden patina under the combined lights of the setting sun and the streetlights and lights in shop windows just coming on.

Clouded glimpses of myself in shop windows showed that I had a little cylindrical hat perched on my head, the same grey as the skirt and coat, but with a dark-red ribbon wound around the edge.

My feet made a click-click sound as I walked, because I was wearing ridiculously high and thin heels. Fortunately, the knowledge that came with the game included the knowledge of how to walk in those.

And I had a dark-red shoulder bag, that I knew without checking contained one of the guns that, as Joe had told me, was then called a "heater." Some kind of primitive ray weapon.

The shop windows I passed, their lights just blinking on, displayed mannequins wearing the latest fashions, or perhaps piles of handbags, or, in one case, delightful pyramids of fanciful pastries.

It was hard to believe this was all made up: the great variety of men—wearing matching hats, pants, and coats, with shirts and ties, all of a style familiar to anyone who'd even seen commercials for Nick Rhodes—walking by, some smiling and tipping their hat at me, and women—all probably better-looking than average, wearing heels as high as mine, and similar costumes, except for those who wore dresses, or maid outfits—walking past and sometimes glaring at me.

The sudden little gusts of wind that whipped the drizzle against my nylon-clad legs felt real. And the noise of the city was amazing: from the continuous purr of motor vehicles, to the random shouting of someone greeting a friend, to music playing from apartments above the shops: all of it seemed real, random, amazing.

At the corner before the house on 35th Street, a truck was unloading bricks, the workers in overalls shouting and gesturing at each other and speaking a dialect I hadn't encountered, with borrow-words that my mersi-self knew were old Italian but couldn't decipher.

One of them whistled and another laughed as I walked by. I crossed the street when the crossing light turned green. On the other side a young man just past the age at which he might legitimately have been called a boy, wearing a cap set sideways on his head, stood by a pile of rolled-up newspapers, and held one open in his right hand, as he shouted, "Read about Nick Rhodes's fabulous feat!"

The headline, printed in reddish-brown ink, said, "Nick Rhodes Solves Satanic Solvent Slaying!"

Three doors down was 454 West 35th Street. It was a rowhouse amid rowhouses, made of golden stone, three floors high, each—except the corner ones—sharing walls with its two neighbors.

The front doors were up a flight of steps, ten in the case of Nick's home, and despite standing hemmed in, they had an opulent feeling.

I climbed the steps in a flurry of castanet sounds from my high heels, and—standing under the tiny little overhang over the door—turned to close my umbrella and shake it, so as not to take water inside.

Before I turned around, much less rang the bell or unlocked the door, the door opened.

Loup Armel didn't look like much. He was about my height—without the heels—golden-skinned, with a narrow, aquiline nose and sharp brown eyes under bushy eyebrows. His straight dark hair had some grey streaks, and his voice had a French accent, as he spoke. "Ah, Miss D'Or. He's waiting for you."

"Oh, but—"

"No, no. He's waiting for you in some anxiety. You know how he gets."

I had no idea how he got, but I had the impression this was standard to the mersi, so I smiled a little, and nodded, as I stepped into the hallway. Loup more or less wrenched the umbrella from me, saying an indistinct string of words, from which "Mon dieu" and "Out in this storm" emerged. Loup Armel, I suddenly knew, was supposed to be a mother-hen who viewed venturing outside the brownstone in anything but perfect halcyon spring weather an adventure not worth experiencing.

The hall in which I was left was...opulent. I wondered if that was part of what had influenced Joe to think that the first few rooms that our clients encountered had to be as rich-looking as we could make them.

The walls of the hall were paneled in rich wood. To my right there was a coat tree in wood and golden metal. There was also an umbrella stand, white and blue, in Chinese style. Why Loup hadn't simply deposited my umbrella there was not a question worth exploring.

To my right was a gilded table, topped in marble, where normally there would be mail deposited. Or packages. It was bare, save for a vase filled with red roses, their fragrance filling the hall.

Above the table hung a mirror in an elaborate rococo frame. Unconsciously, I lifted my hands to fix the chin-length hair that the wind had disarranged, and to remove the pin that held my tiny hat atop my head. I put the hat on the table and finished fixing my hair.

I looked like me. That wasn't a shock, of course. The differences were more important. Instead of my normal blue-grey eyes, I had bright green eyes. I supposed that was a point of characterization for Stella D'Or. And my hair, instead of being light brown, spilling down my back, was now pale blond, cut very short in a sculpted cut.

The rest—

Let's say the mersi enhanced just the things that would make any man appreciative to see me. I'd always looked good, but not this good. I also seemed to move more gracefully than I did, even in my dancing.

The mahogany door next to the mirror opened. A voice spoke from inside. "Stella!" It was a clipped and commanding voice, and I wasn't sure it was Joe's. Perhaps it was the voice I'd heard from the borg.

I opened the door and stepped in. And did a double take. It was our office from the *35th Street,* just a little larger. Joe's desk was there, or an exact replica, leaning against a wall of bookcases—which Joe would love, if he could afford the antique paper books that filled this one—and there was my desk to the right, against the wall, topped with a gleaming black and silver typewriter, a spike with some papers speared through and a wooden copy stand.

But behind Joe's desk, sitting in Joe's favorite position was— Well, it looked like Joe, wearing a mask shaped like the borg's face, which was distracting. The rest was pure Joe, from the unruly dark blond hair, to the square shoulders, narrow waist, and the long legs that came down as he removed his feet from the desk and stood up. He put a book down at the same time. Reflexively I read the title: *What to Do in a Bind?*

Nick was up and walking towards me. "I understand you're in a bind?"

I nodded.

I don't know what I expected Nick to do in the situation. Hug me? I mean, I knew that the entire plot of the mersi was, "Are they, or aren't they?" but surely this was a fanfic made by my husband. Hug me or ask me to pour my troubles into his willing ear.

What he did, instead, was precisely what Joe would do in the circumstances. Which made perfect sense and was also a little insane.

He took me to the basement.

No, I'd never heard of the house on West 35th Street having a basement, either. But in this version, it did. And the basement was a high-tech gun range and gym.

I spent a week subjective time in that basement, which means that time must have been set to run very fast in the mersi, as it was only a few hours in the real world.

In that week, I shot every possible weapon and learned their tricks. Weapons of our time, not of Nick Rhode's time. And I learned free-fighting techniques. And Nick Rhodes, who couldn't possibly know anything about that time, told me very seriously, "For these to work outside the mersi, you must get nano shots. Promise me you'll get strength-enhancing nano-shots, Stella."

I promised.

In both shooting and fighting, I started out being... Well, me. My strengths had absolutely nothing to do with fighting or weapons. But of course, mersis are really good for training reflexes. And we repeated and repeated and repeated.

There were breaks for meals and sleeping. During the meals, Nick talked. Call it "Techniques of Investigation 101," although all of them were geared for our time, not his supposed time. There were hints on where to search for information, which archives were worth it, and which we—I presumed Joe and myself—had subscriptions for. There were discussions about how to interrogate a suspect, which seemed to—at least in my mind—burn down to: if you get them talking, let them talk. Even if you think everything they're telling you is a pack of lies, sooner or later the truth will come out, mixed in, whether they mean to tell it or not. And just a lot of instruction on how to look for contradictions in stories, and in people's body language.

There was also sleep in the mersi, and I have no clue if it was the same subjective eight hours it was supposed to take, but Nick handed me a headband connected to some kind of primitive recording-playing device and told me to listen to it while I slept. I have no idea how much information that transmitted, but again, it was the basics of quick and dirty investigation, what was permissible in most worlds and what might get me in trouble in some. I was in awe of how much data—most of it probably proprietary teaching data—my husband had uploaded into the unit and smuggled aboard the fanfic.

"I suppose you have to go," Nick told me, on the seventh day, over breakfast.

"I should, yes," I said. I had no idea how long I'd been gone, but I worried about what the borg might do, alone in the ship. It hadn't shown any interest in being destructive, certainly not to me. But you never knew.

Nick sighed heavily, a sound so much like Joe when he was frustrated that it was endearing. "I wish we had ten times the time."

"I know," I said, drinking coffee, and eating buttered croissants, which supposing both Joe and I survived this adventure, I was going to ask him to program into the mersi's cooker. "But the situation is dangerous, and I must go back and deal with it."

"I suppose if the situation weren't dangerous, you wouldn't be here. I know that I was programmed for a dire situation. I suppose I— That is, Joe isn't available to help you through this?"

I sighed. "It's complicated," I said. "You might both be available."

"Oh," he said. He looked shocked but not curious, and I wondered at the programming. "Well, then I'll give you some advice. Lean on me, when you can. Even if I'm a fish out of water in your time, I should be able to help."

And like that, he walked me to the door, where he handed me an umbrella and shook my hand. His hand felt exactly like Joe's, and I wanted to hug him.

But instead, I opened the door, and stepped out into the early-morning light drizzle and heavy wind, with the streetlights just going off, and the sun starting to shine, pink and bright over the horizon, and people in antique costumes hurrying to work I couldn't quite believe wasn't really there behind the bright facades of offices and shop windows.

And I woke up, and opened the clamshell. And screamed.

A Friend In Need

The scream came because there was a man in our spare room, close to the unit.

It took blinking hard to recognize Jim, and by then he had started to apologize. "I'm sorry, Lil," he said. "I was trying to see how much time you had left. I presume you were doing research of some sort."

"Of some sort," I said. "Did you see it?"

"Yes," Jim said. "I came up, saw the mersi was engaged, went downstairs to the office—" He stopped, and chewed on the edge of his thumbnail.

"You think it is—"

His eyes were large, horrified. He nodded and shrugged. "I don't know who else it could be, Lil. He... It's the same gestures, all of them." He paused, for a moment in confusion. "He called me both Jim and Alex. I presume that's a Nick Rhodes thing."

"Yes," I said. "I think Joe programmed us all into his Nick Rhodes mersi."

And to Joe's sudden look of alarm, "Well, you know, it's not unusual for hardcore fans."

"I suppose not. Seems strange. But then I'm not a mersi fan."

Normally I'd have agreed, but— This mersi and Joe's habits might yet save my life.

I went to the office, with Joe following close. The borg was at Joe's desk, reading the book that Joe had laid aside. The one by Narkissus Humel.

He put it down when we approached, in a gesture much like Joe's. And Nick Rhodes, for that matter.

"I have to go out for a few hours or a few days," I said. And on a sudden flash of inspiration, because after all it was Joe's brain in there, or it probably was, added, "It relates to the Emergency Sequence."

The damn borg didn't have eyebrows. He certainly couldn't raise them. And yet somehow he did, this also so much like Joe's expressions it hurt. "I see," he said. "I'll stay here till you return."

And as we headed out the door, in reverse order, with Jim leading, he added, "Alex, take care of Stella."

Jim grunted something that sounded affirmative, and we were in the hallway, and Jim was opening the door to the airlock, which had another airlock perma-latched on.

We closed the door to the inside, then stepped into the other interstellar, and Jim closed the door to my ship, before closing his own and stepping in, to allow the airlock to cycle, and the two ships to disengage.

It was only then that it occurred to me to ask how he'd gotten in without my opening the door. "I've had the unlock sequences since Joe married," he said. And with a preoccupied and apologetic smile, "He wanted me to have it in the case of an emergency."

I nodded.

This interstellar was far more luxurious than ours. Also, it was decorated in a certain...style. For one, there was no entrance hall, no offices, no work rooms of any sort. What there was consisted of a giant...socializing room. Okay, okay, a party room, decorated in red velvet with crystal chandeliers. It had low velvet sofas, what looked damn well like a bed fit for six in a corner, and the vastest, glitteriest glass bar I've ever seen next to the bed. I didn't have time to examine all the cubicles above the bar, but from the shape and color of the bottles, there was an amazing selection of liquors, some of them possibly illegal in most worlds.

Jim cleared his throat. "Do you need a drink?"

I shook my head. "Need, yes. Have one, no."

He cackled. "Oh, I get that."

And when I asked, "Jim, it's your privacy and all, but how in hell's name did you acquire an unregistered interstellar bordello?" I was starting to think that the surprising thing was not that we'd had to extricate this man from possibly the strangest sexual adventure in the history of humanity, but it was that we'd never had to do more than that.

His laugh was embarrassed. "It's not mine. I just know people who have it, and I... Well, I knew how to ask."

"Blackmail, Jim?"

He laughed openly this time. "Oh, you have no idea what mediators of news do, do you, sweetheart? All is ours to conceal and reveal. Or almost all. Okay, what do you want to do, and what can I do for you?"

I explained. His eyes acquired a faraway glimmer as I explained I needed a good cosmetics person, with the capacity to make some minor body modifications.

For a moment I thought he was going to tell me he didn't know anyone like that, but what he asked was more cogent and to the point. "Isn't it strange to go around looking like Stella D'Or? I take it as written that Joe—if he's not the brain in the borg, and Lil, I'm afraid he is—would instantly recognize you in that getup, but so would a lot of other people. And the Global War One might take it pretty hard that you're running around impersonating one of its copyrighted characters."

I giggled. "No, I won't be. Stella, the original Stella, doesn't look a thing like me, Jim. Much taller, and completely different features. Even the haircut is different. I've seen the commercials. As far as I can tell, the only thing that Stella has in common with the Stella that Joe programmed is the green eyes. Which I'll need to acquire, of course."

"Of course," he said, and frowned. "A moment."

He went into a small room on the side, which he said was coms. Minutes later, he came back. "I know just where to take you."

If I hadn't trusted Jim with my very life... Of course I trusted Jim with my very life. If Joe trusted him with the codes to the *35th Street*, there was nothing for me to suspect, even if the lessons so recently impressed in the mersi session told me not to trust anyone, and never to let myself be led to a place I didn't know.

But in this case, I had to trust Jim, even if I watched him like a hawk, just in case he had some sudden and strange idea of treachery. After all, you know, if Joe and I were both dead, then Jim would have disposed of the last two people who knew anything about his strange adventures in gengineering. On the other hand—

On the other hand, no. It didn't fit. If Jim wanted to dispose of both of us, it would have been easier to borrow a ship with weaponry—which certainly someone who had access to the flying bordello would be able to get—and use it to blast the *West 35th Street* to dust in the middle of nowhere.

No.

As it was, I was right to trust Jim. We didn't land, but locked onto a habitat in another nowhere. I was versed enough in the history of interstellar navigation to know it was actually an abandoned node.

Joe and I had often, idly, browsed through the listings for the resale of such habitats. They were spherical...islands, would be a good way to put it. Once upon a time they anchored nodes from which ships could transition to other nodes. In the days when the human-link to the computer first stopped being needed, ships could only do short jumps.

When the technology changed, these jump-point node anchors, which were usually the size of a small village or a large homestead, and had once contained shops, homes and sometimes schools and interesting museums, were suddenly left outside the flow of normal ship jumps, forgotten and off the navigational charts.

They were sold, whenever the technology took another jump and another one of them emptied. Sometimes, I understood, they were simply abandoned, and within a century or two someone claimed them as a squatter or a new owner, if you consider that possession is everywhere nine-tenths of the law.

I suspected this one had been abandoned and reclaimed. For one, it looked very old. Likely more than a thousand years old. It had that archaic feel in its design.

The things were nearly indestructible by design, since in normal times tens of thousands of lives would depend on it, maintained or not.

As our interstellar maneuvered to dock at what had once been one of many "welcome airlocks" but which was now clearly the only operational one, I saw a name painted over the area: "Golden Harbor." It was done in fancy gold script and might once have been in some kind of emissive material. If it had once had the same name.

Jim maneuvered us to docking, then pressed a code sequence into our own ship's transmitter. I found this fascinating, since if this were a place of high business, almost for sure they would require contact or meeting in advance.

Instead, it seemed to be the sort of "we're open to friends" places that are fairly sure no one will be there to feel inconvenienced if you trample in unannounced.

There was a long delay, and then the lock outside our airlock processed, filling with air, and our lock opened. Jim looked over his shoulder, to make sure I was following.

I don't know what I expected. I know I didn't expect farm country. Nor did I expect to walk down a dirt path amid tall bean plants to find a row of shorter bean plants, and a man who looked about my father's age staking them and tying them to the stakes. As we approached, he removed a bunch of the ties from his mouth—which every human seems to use as a third hand in need—and grinned at us. He had perfect teeth. His dark hair had only a few threads of grey. He wore faded blue coveralls. And though there wasn't a single feature in common, and he was shorter, I got the impression that he was related to Jim. "Hi, Jim," he said. "I didn't expect to see you anytime soon. It's hard enough to get you to holo, much less leave New Oxford."

Jim smiled. It was the type of smile he gave when he didn't really want to talk about it. "Hi, Paul." Turning to me, he said, "Lil, this is Paul. Paul, Lil needs a... Makeover. Stat."

The man's eyebrows went up as he looked me over. "Would be a pity to change the features."

"The features don't really need to change," I said.

"But the DNA should, at least temporarily. Just in case her features ping something."

The eyebrows went up further. He looked from me to Jim. "Oh, I see. Hot?"

I was about to open my mouth and say that while the character could be considered sexy, that wasn't the main purpose of it, but Jim said, "Boiling."

Paul made a sound like "uh." Then he carefully set his ties inside one of the plants he'd finished with, put the stakes on the ground, wiped his hands on his coveralls, and said, "Come with me."

We walked past a field of tall corn, and one of wheat. The light in the artificial sky was that of late summer or early autumn at sunset.

We passed features I suspect were there when this place was a hub, and likely beset with shops and public attractions. At least I can't figure out any other reason why, after the cornfield, there was a glassteel-but-looking-like-rustic-stone arched bridge over a babbling brook. And then the dirt path continued. We came eventually to a farmhouse, straight out of what the holos show for late nineteenth-century Earth: sprawling, rectangular, white. There was a barn to one side of it, and from somewhere came the sound of clucking chickens.

A big dog came to greet us as we approached. Paul looked over his shoulder at Jim. "Hazel isn't in. She's doing a supply run."

And the door opened itself, and despite the rustic exterior, the interior of the farmhouse was completely up to date, from plush bio-carpet, the kind that kept itself clean, to sculpted wood furniture in sleek shapes.

Our host took his shoes off at the entrance, and we followed suit.

He guided us to a room set with low couches. Paul—who, I later found out, was a doctor in multiple disciplines—asked me what I wanted to look like. I explained the whole "just bright green eyes," and how my hair should be a certain length and my body definitely should change. More here, less there. Just enough to take me from decent-looking to amazing. He nodded. And took notes.

After a while, he looked at Jim. "But why keep the same features, if—"

"She needs to be recognized. And also, who is going to imagine she'd go through the trouble to create all the differences, but keep the same face?"

Paul nodded. "There is a certain sense in that. Now, the DNA, I take it not permanent?"

I shook my head. Mind you, I knew next to nothing about how deep DNA changes went. I knew it was possible to change the DNA in everything you shed, from body fluids to hair and skin cells, but I wasn't sure what difference that made to who you were. I also knew the most complete sorts of DNA modifications changed everything about you, but your brain. And I knew those were permanent.

"Good. Temp is easy. And on external and shed-only. That's easy. After that you get into rejection issues, and—" He shrugged and gave us a grin. "It's almost as illegal as borging and for the same reasons. It renders you sterile, for one. And the most complete kind of change, the one that does everything but your brain? You'll need to take anti-rejection drugs the rest of your life. The appearance is permanent, though? Because that's easiest. It's just cosmetic regen."

And then... Well, and then we went into a lab. I was injected with things, and eventually put to sleep and immersed in a tank. It was, as I later learned, a regen tank with certain very specific properties.

Jim tells me I was in the tank for about five hours. While I was in the tank, asleep, immersed in regen fluid, I was subjected to a series of mersi tapes with hypnotic properties.

You might not realize it, but how you move and walk and run are all part of the function of your body size and design. This is why children and particularly teenagers so often appear clumsy and accident-prone. When your body size and mass and design are changing all the time, you don't know how to move without bumping into things, toppling things, or falling.

The hypno made sure I moved as though my body had always been this size and shape, as though the smaller waist and larger, heavier breasts had always been there.

When I came out of the regen tank, I was alone in the room, and there was a robe hanging on the wall. This led me out into another room, which had a full-length mirror. I think they were afraid that I'd be shocked and wanted me to have time to integrate my new appearance.

But it wasn't new. I looked like Stella D'Or in the mersi. That was fine. I could deal with that. Even the walking took me back to the mersi.

There was in fact a certain reassurance in it. In the mersi, Joe had been alive. Or he'd been alive in a way. Maybe he was still alive in a way, but was I prepared to live with a Joe made of glassteel?

I walked my way out of the room, in the graceful steps required by my new shape.

They were waiting for me in the living room. Paul gave instructions, which mostly amounted to what I called "Cinderella rules"—as in, don't be caught anywhere public where you could end up dead if your DNA is sequenced. Other than that, I was free to go. The DNA I'd been given as a "shedding DNA" was previously nonexistent, but had been introduced in a lot of databases as Stella D'Or. Which would probably confuse the hell out of any fan of the show, but hopefully not till long after I was done with this case.

And Joe was safely back in Elysium, having found a bolt-hole, I hoped but did not believe. And if he were, he'd see me and contact me. And we'd be together again.

This is what the current gambit was all about.

Apparently while I was being modified, Jim and the doctor had worked up a wardrobe for my new shape. It must have been an all-needs-stop for a lot of people.

The wardrobe was not like in the game in that it was a contemporary one. And though the Rhodes mersi had influenced fashion, and dresses and skirts were de-rigueur in many worlds, no one wore the sky-high, thin-heeled shoes that Stella wore.

"All the clothes are in your room," Jim said, and walked me through the bordello-like large room to a private room about the size of a good-sized closet: enough for a double bed, and built-in drawers and closets, where the clothes were.

I must have looked my confusion, because Jim laughed. "This place requires private rooms, you know, for...private activities."

I didn't dispute it, but again, I suspected my friend had far more interesting connections and background than Joe or I had ever dared suspect.

"I'll be in the room next door." He hesitated. "I do suggest you rest. I assume you want to make your way back to Elysium?"

And when I nodded, he said, "I've looked at databases while you were under, and no one links me or you to this ship. So, we should be able to land and have you go out. Do you have any idea what you want to do in Elysium?"

"I want to see Joe's Aunt Arana," I said. "Because he saw her, and there might have been something in the encounter, though he didn't tell me what. I'd also like you—if you can—to see if you can find anything else about Narkissus's two wives that Uncle Gul knew of." I paused. "Is Uncle Gul still alive? Has he woken?"

"He's alive and he hasn't woken. I have trackers on that, and the first whisper of news will get reported to me." He smiled. I think he thought it was reassuring. And to be honest, he probably was trying to be reassuring. But I could tell he was nervous about this whole thing because he'd been doing something to his hair. I imagine he'd been running his hand through it, over and over again. That would account for the way his hair looked like a stormy sea, all random waves and strange, unexpected peaks.

"It will take about twenty-four hours to get to Elysium from where we are. We're taking a circuitous series of jumps, so it's not obvious where we're coming from—Paul wouldn't like that—and frankly so no one knows where we're headed. Or at least we don't call undue attention. It's less likely they will connect your features with you if we do not make it too obvious. Anyway, I suggest you use the time to rest and make up your mind about precisely what you want to accomplish in Elyseum." I nodded and he continued, "I'll run the search for Idelle Zay and Raine Chlo. Neither of them seem to be anywhere that can be traced." He looked worried. "But—if one of them surfaces, I'll wake you."

I nodded, and as he started to walk away, I said, "Jim?"

He turned back, eyebrows raised.

"Who is doing your news aggregating while you're here? Isn't it an all-the-time job?"

He made a face, but there was a quirk of the lips that told me he was actually amused. "Well, it would be," he said. "If I let it. But even newspeople have to eat and sleep, and have the occasional day off. I have assistants, and also a very sophisticated AI that can make the same decisions I make about nine times out of ten. I just review the decisions, and am still doing so while here. Cloaked, of course. For all anyone knows, I'm in my apartment in New Oxford."

And then he was gone, and I tried to sleep. I thought I wouldn't manage it, with everything going around and around in my mind, from the fact that Jim had criminal associations, and I should probably be thankful for that, considering he might otherwise refuse to associate with me, to the fact that he knew someone who did appearance and DNA modification. From the quick refresh on interplanetary law

I'd gotten in the mersi, I knew that he was now as implicated in a capital case of borging as I was. Both of us would get death if caught. But DNA disguising was equally illegal. The various governments of various worlds, no matter how different, all agreed on one thing: people should not be able to disappear from the radar and stop being traced. Because that denied government's ability to identify troublemakers and rebels, criminals and those who simply wanted to be left alone. And that would not be permitted.

With that thought in mind, I fell asleep and had a thoroughly unpleasant dream in which Joe's Auntie Arana was a borg and was talking to me about the joys of being a borg, or, as she put it, leaving the flesh behind.

I woke up with Jim shouting, "Lilly!"

I was sitting bolt upright, eyes wide open, ready to fight or flee, when I realized that Jim was smiling. "I found Idelle Zay," he said.

"You..."

"Well, found her is a manner of speaking. I have no idea where she is. She's guarding her location somehow, but she is willing to talk to us, in holo, in a connection through about a hundred proxies. I'm to give a signal when we're ready, and I think we should do it as soon as possible, just in case one of the favors I pulled in changes his mind."

I nodded, reading between the lines.

Twenty minutes later, I was freshed, dressed in a fancy blue satin suit with a skirt over tight pants and a tunic over the whole of it, which shouldn't have looked good but did.

We were in the main portion of the intergalactic bordello, each of us sitting on one of the more proper chairs: sure, studded red leather, but small. I assumed they were display chairs for ladies of negotiable virtue, but then I knew almost nothing of what went on in such places and in such situations.

Jim had given his signal. He had also gotten a notepad and a pencil. Yes, real retro ones. Paper or a decent facsimile thereof, and graphite enclosed in wood. It seemed like a very weird affectation for a man who was, if anything, extremely practical. I started to wonder if I'd ever actually known anyone, as Jim crossed one leg over the other, and held the pencil poised over the pad which rested on his knee.

I don't know what signal he gave, but I got to—for the first time—see a holo obviously re-directed several times over, from place to place. It was like flickers of things materialized in the center of the room. Not people, things. Though sometimes it included a portion of someone. You know, a corner of a room, a chair, and someone's knee, and then it dissolved, and it was another room, a different chair, or a cylindrical, egg-white room, with polished walls, or—

There were about seven flickers of similar things, one of them I would swear was a view out of a window that seemed startlingly similar to the view from my room in Father's home at Elfenheim.

And then, suddenly, all the more startlingly because of the previous confusion, a woman materialized in the center of the room.

She was sitting in a white armchair, with something red draped under her. She wore a black dress, severely tailored and she was—

Beautiful. As Uncle Gul had said, she was tall and slim and blond, all pale, but a paleness that had a touch of gold, like some very old, polished ivory of the kind that used to be imported from Kyre and made into vases—until it was discovered it was probably what remained of sentient beings, since it came from a world littered with the remains of sentient-being technology. She was like that: a very pale gold, very smooth, and behind it a feeling that she was too polished, too exact. A tool made by someone. Or perhaps what remained of a long-ago sentient being, now utterly lost and alien.

Her hair, too, looked like very pale spun gold, but it was when she raised her eyes to us that I realized that she wasn't quite human. I don't know how to explain it. I mean, she was undeniably a member of the homo sapien species, but then again you got a feeling that what of her was normal and mortal—the part of her that could have cradled a baby, laughed with a friend, danced with a lover—was gone. That all that was left was...whatever remains when that was lost.

And yet, her dark amber eyes were full of fire and force, of purpose, or something driven and intent.

"I was told," she said, "that you wished to speak to me. That the matter somehow involves my ex-husband? Narkissus?" Her voice was low for a woman's, but more than that, it seemed to have an embedded purr. It wasn't as though she was trying to be sexy. It was more like this was simply the way she talked. There was a trace of an accent there, but I wasn't sure what it might be or where it had come from.

"Yes," I said. I realized my mind was finding and discarding what I should tell her. How I should tailor our enquiry so she would consider helping us, if indeed she had something that could help us. That alone was hard to figure out, as I wasn't sure what she would be able to tell us. I was groping in the dark without direction, and with only the vaguest hope that something—anything—related to Narkissus Humel might help.

"You see, Narkissus retired to a place called Elysium," I said.

She didn't say anything, but minimally raised her left shoulder, in a backward semi-circular motion that seemed to ask why she was supposed to care about that.

"Uncle Gul— Gulbahar Felix helped him settle." Was it my imagination that when I mentioned Uncle Gul, her face became very intent, almost as if she'd just woken up? "And on his way back from Elysium, Uncle Gul found that his interstellar had been tampered with. He barely managed to make it work, but not before he got a view of the world closest to the sun, a world filled with borgs." Something flickered in her eyes, but I couldn't tell what, whether disgust or disbelief.

Aloud, she said, "Gul is your uncle?"

"Not...biological, but yes, that is what I've called him since I can remember."

She quirked her lip and looked me over, frowning slightly. Then nodded.

"Anyway, Uncle Gul said he got messages from Narkissus Humel, saying that he felt threatened, or that people were dying out of order, or something like that. And then Narkissus died, and he shouldn't have died that early. Then Uncle Gul found the messages gone from his house, and then he was attacked. He's...unconscious. Between life and death, I was told."

She nodded, as though to say she knew that part. And that voice, almost a purr, said, "Now tell me what the problem is. The whole story. All of it. Please. I know it's way more complicated than that. Whatever involves Narkissus always is."

"But if I tell you..." I looked sideways at Jim, who was writing furiously on his notepad, while looking at Idelle. Idelle followed my eyes and smiled. Just a little smile, and a tip of the head, and Jim returned it.

It was the oddest thing. Have you ever lived through one of those mersis that are supposedly set in Earth's era of high chivalry? Where before going after each other with swords and deadly intent, duelists will salute each other with all civility? Well, that's what this was like.

"I do not know who you are," Idelle said. "I know who that gentleman is, if nothing else because it would take his kind of connected power to be able to get to me, where I was hiding, but perhaps this is not him, but a deep fake. Perhaps I am not able to tell if it's the real Jim Brighton." She leaned forward. I thought she must be close to two hundred. Or at least Jim thought she must be close to two hundred, if not older. But she didn't look it. Instead, she looked—ageless. And definitely like an attractive woman. Though at the same time I got the feeling that she wasn't trying to be attractive, that she simply didn't care anymore, except about things having nothing to do with having a body. "Tell me," she said.

And like that, I told her. I told her the whole thing, starting with the airlock chiming, then backtracking to Uncle Gul's call on us to solve the case of his old friend.

She joined her hands in steeple and listened. She was so still, one started to wonder if she was in fact still breathing. But if you looked closely, you saw her chest moving, minimally.

It was disturbing, as though she'd been turned to stone by my story.

When I was done, she started at me a long time. "Truly? You couldn't trace where Narkissus came from?"

"No," I said. "His DNA on file doesn't trace to any place we can find. And we can't find where he graduated from. And yet New Oxford took him."

The silence went on. Idelle looked up, as though there were something fascinating in the ceiling above her. Perhaps there was. She was an artist, after all. And the holo showed us only her sitting in a chair, not the room she was in. Perhaps the ceiling had some kind of installation.

Then she said, "Mister Brighton, how secure is this linkage?"

James came to life, as if jolted. I hadn't realized he too had been unnaturally still until that moment. "The people who put us in touch told us your life might depend on keeping your location secret, so it is very secure."

Idelle pursed her lips. All of her gestures were carefully deliberate, so that I wondered if they were natural, or part of a contrived attempt to fool us. But if they were an attempt to fool us, she'd surely make them seem more natural. No. Her gestures were rather those of someone who over a very long time had learned to discipline herself so that—

And there I stopped, not sure what the *so that* was.

Which was good, because just as I gave up on guessing her motives, she began to speak. "When I met Narkissus, he had just arrived in New Oxford from Ufraglio."

There was a long silence, and I kept expecting Jim to say something, having described his own origins in a world that appeared to have been designed for criminal activities. But he said nothing.

"He was, as you would be later, Mr. Brighton, a scholarship student. The dons of New Oxford live forever in the abiding hope that if they get in enough students from Ufraglio, eventually Ufraglio itself will reform." She laughed, but it was a sound without mirth. "I am a student of history, you know, and that illusion has remarkably long roots, the idea that if only people are sufficiently educated, they will stop having—or at least obeying—their baser impulses and desires."

By the corner of my eye, I saw Jim make a reflexive movement, as though to refute it.

"Oh, I'm not disputing completely," she said. "For some like you, and arguably Narkissus, there is hope. There is a desire to leave the confused half-light world behind and step into...legality and legal recognition.

"Narkissus was like that. We were both students at the same time, he in criminal justice, and I in art. We fell in love, got married, and in the fullness of time left New Oxford to find our place in the world. My art was at first soundly ignored, and Narkissus taught at a lot of small colleges. Then my art started paying, though not much. For ten years we lived in Far Itravine, near my family, where the living is cheap, and we could pay for a small beach cottage from my meager earnings.

"Then he got his offer to teach at New Oxford, as an adjunct at first. By then we'd been married thirty years and I thought perhaps we might want to have children, but Narkissus was violently opposed to the idea. He said when you're from Ufraglio, if you have children, you're making them hostages to fortune." She paused. "You see, he says it's all bloodlines, and wars carried out over several generations, and—and people to whom you owe things."

By the corner of my eye, I saw Jim nod, an almost imperceptible movement. I wondered what the strings on him were. Then I thought of Paul and the magic worked on me, and how illegal that must be and in how many worlds.

Strings. Ties. People to whom you owe things. I got that.

"Narkissus was afraid that if we had children, our children or grandchildren or even great-grandchildren would one day, somehow, be extorted with something relating to the bloodline. That their position in the world would be imperiled, or that they would otherwise be threatened, unless they did things they did not wish to do.

"So, children never happened. I had some idea they might happen at some time, in the future, in some future marriage. But my art became better known, and I started traveling to exhibits, and to talk, and Narkissus advanced in his career.

"We settled in a comfortable pattern for some decades." She stopped and looked surprised, for a moment, as though she'd just realized something. "That was when we met Gulbahar Felix. We used to have parties. I found his mind stimulating. For a time, I thought—"

She shrugged and went on. "And then our life was turned on its head. One of those...ties from Ufraglio. Someone came to Narkissus. They talked. He told me that it would be dangerous to stay married. And we divorced. And he married Raine Chlo." There was a long silence. "I think if you run Raine Chlo's DNA you'll also find it's untraceable."

She sighed. "Well, after that, I didn't know much about him, until this last year. I got a message from him that... Well, I can't explain it. If someone else had read it, they would have thought it was a casual message, sent from a vacationing couple. But there were... You can't be married to someone for that long without having all kinds of inside jokes and comments, and other...things the other spouse understands. And I understood. It seemed to be a cry for help from Narkissus. He said he was being held against his will."

A pause, a little longer than I expected. "And then the death threats started. And the attempted assassinations. I've been in hiding ever since."

We thanked her and disconnected. There wasn't much more we could do and say. I sensed she might have known more than she told us, but if so, we lacked the ability to make her tell us more, so there was no point.

Jim did the thanking, a profuse, respectful torrent, and I wondered if it was in deference to her name in the art world, or her bank account, or—for that matter—her Ufraglio connections through Narkissus. And those Ufraglio connections were obviously a problem.

Look, one jokes about corrupt worlds and the criminal nets they spread throughout the rest of the human worlds, but— Even if I had never heard of Ufraglio, or perhaps because I had never heard of Ufraglio, not in conversations at Father's house, and not while working with Joe, perhaps Ufraglio was more dangerous than all the worlds we knew about.

After Jim turned off the connection to the holo, I blinked owlishly at him. "I think," I said, as much to see Jim's expression as to say it, "that Narkissus Humel had the same thing done that I just had done."

Jim's eyes went wide, but his lips twisted in something not quite a smile. "Well, obviously," he said. "It might even have been with Paul, not that he'd ever tell us."

I nodded. "So?" I said.

To which Jim answered with the strangest thing I'd ever heard. "Lilly, how much did you know about Joe?"

I blinked at him. "I'm married—at least I hope I'm still married—to him."

He made a gesture like someone drawing aside a curtain, a mix of impatience and annoyance. "Yes, but." He started pacing across the ridiculously decorated main area of the ship. "Seriously. How much did you know about him and his background?"

"I knew he had training in private investigations and was certified for work across all the human worlds, or at least all of them who recognize interplanetary law. And I knew he loved dancing and was very good at it, particularly tango. Oh, and I knew that he liked to cook gourmet food, and that he hated being tied down to a job for too long, and that—"

"Sure." Jim ran his hand back through his short and choppy hair, creating something I believe would be considered an avant-garde hairstyle in many worlds. "But I didn't mean that. I meant, what do you know about his family and where he grew up?"

I stared at Jim. Joe had been remarkably good at avoiding all mention of his past. All the reminiscences I'd heard before this case were about things like "my mom loved to cook." But never personal names, times, places. When I could command my mouth to work, I said, "Damn it, Jim, if you tell me that he was born and raised in Ufraglio, I'm going to kill someone."

He grinned. "Not that I know of. That would be one hell of a mod. He's too pale and blond." He shook his head. "I guess what I'm trying to ask you is: had you ever heard of someone called Valli Arana in his family before?"

I shook my head. "No. It was just before we went to Elysium, he said he'd found he had an aunt there. His grandmother's sister."

"Lilly, I've been looking into Valli Arana's past. She has no children, no siblings. She worked as a private detective long ago, when she was young...but she has no living family, and certainly not Joe. And Joe... You know... I don't know how to put this to you, but he is a man without a past."

"Again, Jim, if he is from Ufraglio—"

Jim shook his head. "No. I don't think there's anything that simple in his past. Truly. I looked him up, you know, when I first hired him, before he married you. And all my resources, and all my looking couldn't find Joe younger than sixteen, when he blew into New Oxford for training. He financed it by selling a lot of old books in an amazing state of preservation. He gave his birthplace as a decaying orbital station, a place like the one where Paul lives, and his parents as deceased." His hand went back through his hair again. "It's possible, of course. People are born in such places, and eventually decide to join civilization. In the first diaspora of human colonization, between lost colonies, abandoned trade stations, and people who don't feel safe unless they're as far away from everyone as possible, there are a lot of places people can come from without it showing up on records anywhere. The only thing strange about Narkissus Humel's lack of a past was the fact that he obviously had to have been trained somewhere, at some time. He had to, to teach in New Oxford. His is the incomplete erasure of a past that catches the eye, you know? But I think Joe is something else. And I don't know what it is: isolated cult colony, or lost world-ship, but I—I don't think he's the great-nephew of Valli Arana. I don't think she has any great-nephews."

I tried to process it. "What if her past was also imperfectly erased? What if that's all it was?"

He sighed. "It's possible, but not probable. Her background has no breaks. It also has no link to Joe. I'm telling you because...because there's a good chance of your getting hurt, of you running into trouble."

I wanted to tell him that Joe wouldn't lie to me, but Joe would. Oh, not in personal matters, not in anything that pertained to me, but when a case was going forward, and there was something he wanted me to believe, or something he was afraid I'd reveal if I knew? He'd lie and not think twice. He might tell me the truth later, when the case was solved, the problem and the danger past. But before that? Ah, no.

It didn't make any difference. "I still have to go to Elysium," I explained to Jim. "You see, he went there last. If he's alive but disabled or has gone to ground due to some terrible threat, so terrible that he didn't dare come out even to respond to a danger signal from me, this is my last chance of getting him to come out. That's what the mod was all about. He'll recognize that I'm trying to look like Stella D'Or in his mersi. And he'll come to me if he can. He'll recognize me."

Jim nodded, once, a vigorous movement of his head, and I knew that he knew or thought he knew that Joe was really borged and in the *35th Street*. I wasn't about to say he wasn't, either, but—

But one fights while one can fight. One doesn't give up. One doesn't bend to the inevitable until it is inevitable.

Jim was silent a long time, then said, "But must you go see Valli Arana?"

"Yes, because Joe saw her last. Perhaps there's something in what she said, or in what he told her. So, I have to see her. But I guess I don't have to tell everyone I'm there to see her."

He waggled his head side to side, which is what he did when he was in deep thought, and it seemed to give the impression he was conceding a point. "Sure," he said. "Which means we should give you an identity and a reason to be there. But—" He frowned. "You go rest. I can rest when we've landed in Elysium. In the meantime, I'll check all the background of Valli Arana. There has to be a reason Joe picked her. He wouldn't do it at random. And—" Another frown. "And I'll try to find out more about Elysium, also. When I looked because Joe asked me, I found the normal tangle of torturous connections, corporations and hidden links to shadowy figures, but nothing out of the ordinary. Now, though, I'm starting to wonder. If Gulbahar Felix was right—If there is borging with mining at the nearby giant planet, and possibly others, for rare compounds, well... It could very well be that this is much, much bigger than we thought. And if Ufraglio is involved, well—"

I got up and started back towards the bedroom, then stopped and turned around. "Jim?"

"Yes?"

"You're from Ufraglio."

"Guilty as charged."

"Do you agree with the idea that anyone from there might be...called back, brought back into play by connections from the world at any time?"

He laughed. It was a half-embarrassed laugh. "To an extent." He shook his head. "To an extent, but not— Look, my family wasn't powerful or influential. And I got them out. Every last one of them. I got them out, got them new identities, and dispersed them. For the important people, though? The members of the powerful families with many cousins and numberless connections? Well—" The hand went back through the hair. "Yeah, getting away could be near impossible, and it could take a lot to get away. Also, you know my influence, disproportionate as it is, is limited. As a news aggregator, I can pick what people in all the human worlds see and believe, but as we learned from the news aggregators in Earth's twentieth and twenty-first centuries, you can't impose a completely fictitious reality on humans for too long. They come to realize it and resent it. And then they will never trust you again. So, at most they could ask me to change minor things. For the record, no one has. But they could. However, with a degree in something like criminology, Narkissus would know all the loopholes in laws in various worlds, and—" He was silent a long while. "There was a holo of Narkissus in the past faculty page of New Oxford. If no one has erased it yet, I can do a features search with hereditary parameters enabled for most likely features. Because if he was that scared, he's from one of the important families in Ufraglio."

He turned back, and by the time I closed the door to my temporary room, he was already sitting at the terminal and calling queries faster than I could even think. Which I suppose is why he was good at his difficult, data-driven job.

When I woke up later, we were landing. I know we were landing, because I always felt it, even if you could barely feel it in a ship this size, the forces diffused over all the space, dampened by the thick red carpet, the padded furniture and whatever else was built to keep the passengers comfortable.

I got dressed in the costume that most resembled the things that Stella D'Or would wear: a red dress that looked like silk and was embroidered all over with tiny dragons. The high heels were not as punitive as the ones in the mersi looked. They had cushioning or support of some sort. They made me taller, and made my legs look good, but some kind of cushioning mechanism made me walk effortlessly in them.

Fully dressed, I hid two zappers, one in a thigh holster, the other in a hidden pocket on my gown. Then I examined myself in front of the mirror. Yes, unless Joe had completely lost his memory, if he saw me in Elysium, he would recognize me. Because I looked kind of like Stella D'Or, but mostly I looked like the strange fusion of Stella D'Or and myself that he'd modified the mersi to show. It was a good choice as a signal to him, since it was a private thing between the two of us, like that letter Idelle Zay said she'd received.

I came out of the room to find that Jim had worked himself up to a fine state. And I wasn't sure what his state was, precisely, but only that it was distressing. He was pacing back and forth, and he looked like— He looked as though he'd found out something he didn't like which required that he do something he liked even less, like he was nerving himself up for something.

He spun around mid-walk through the common area when he heard my door open, and said, "Lilly, you can't go."

I frowned at him. "I have to go. Why can't I go?"

"I found out who Valli Arana is." He lifted both hands, in response to what must have been a champion glare from me. "Okay, okay, we already knew who she was. But I found out— She attended the private eye training in New Oxford when I think Narkissus was a student there also. I sent a question out through the connections to Idelle Zay, and she confirmed those were the same years, and as a bonus said that

Narkissus's girlfriend, when he met Idelle and dumped her, was named Valli. She doesn't remember the last name."

"That makes sense," I said. "Joe would have figured it out, I presume, and that's why he went to talk to her. He had to talk to someone who knew Narkissus. No point otherwise."

Jim made a sound of exasperation, and both his hands went up and back through his hair, giving himself a sort of ersatz wings. "Yes, but—" He went back to the controls of the system he'd been using to search. The controls were resting in a small table next to the chair he'd used for our interview with Idelle. He pushed some buttons and faces started materializing mid-air. It was a disturbing experience, because it was as if all these people had forgotten to have a body. Their faces materialized mid-air like so many leavings of a revolution, minus pikes.

It took me a second to realize that all the faces flashing in and out of existence mid-air had a vague family resemblance. Aquiline noses, unruly air, blue eyes that bulged just a little and—

Jim stopped on a particular face. It had all those attributes, and a vaguely amiable smile, though the more I looked at it, the more I got the impression that the amiable smile was pasted on and didn't reach the singularly cold and calculating blue eyes.

I tried to speak, and cleared my throat. "Narkissus?"

"Yeah," Jim said. He moved that holo aside, leaving it suspended in mid-air.

Then he flipped through very rapidly again, features with a vague resemblance to Narkissus flitting by, as though they were cards shuffled by a mad gambler.

One face emerged and Jim stopped. He glared at the face that glared back at him, one with more marked lines than Narkissus, and without attempting even a smile, amiable or not. "This is Alfion Luzend." He looked over his shoulder at me, and smiled slightly, as though finding it amusing that I had not the slightest idea who this might be, as I'm sure my blank face showed. "Head of the Luzend clan, arguably the wealthiest and most powerful in Ufraglio."

"Oh. And those other faces?"

"The Luzend clan," he said. "Which is allied to the Adrealind Clan..." A face appeared on the screen, a woman who looked beautiful, until you caught that the expression was hard enough to cut diamonds. "Lucrella Adrealind, according to my program that predicts the inheritable features, is probably Narkissus's mother. Not that she was ever married to Alfion, but there were...rumors, always. There still are. Lucrella is the head of the Adrealind clan, you see, and they mostly have a friendly relationship with the Luzend clan. Mostly, I say, because there are skirmishes and occasional massacres, but those seem to be the exceptions and the two clans... Well, they go together like untreated syphilis and madness. They run several operations together, from contraband to transportation of fissionable materials, and that's just what can be found on a cursory look."

"I notice none of those names is Humel," I said.

Jim shook his head. "No, of course not. The minute he got that scholarship, he'd have filed a name change in Galactic records, because he was hoping he'd gotten away for good and all."

"Brighton?" I said and raised an eyebrow, which I want to register for the record was the first time in my life that I could do so. It simply wasn't something Lilly could do. I guess Stella had the ability to do it.

He chuckled, "It's not a surname present in Ufraglio—which was, of course, one of its great attractions."

"I'm sure," I said, keeping my voice cold.

"Lilly, I'm serious. Look at these faces. Because I think these clans are involved in whatever is going on up to the eyebrows or a little beyond. And if they are, what you're about to do is probably unimaginably stupid. Or brave. If there is any difference."

I thought about it. I could see his point of view. At least I thought I could. But it didn't make any difference. Joe and I had gotten married by the old rites. He'd insisted on it. To register your marriage, all you needed to do was register it. And if you felt the need to utter vows, you usually made them up on the spot. And no one, *no one,* ever swore "till death do us part."

Sure, historians and sociologists viewed that as a sign of decadence, which they said had set in during the twenty-first century, and they weren't wrong.

The thing is, by our time, it wasn't just decadence. When the average lifespan was around three hundred or so years, longer if you were very rich or very powerful, getting married till death parted you only made sense if you were in your last decades of your third century. Because humans change.

They change too much over a few decades for anyone sane to expect a marriage to work for centuries.

But Joe had demanded the old rites, and the old vows. I'd viewed it as some kind of nostalgia, and gone along with it. Frankly, at the time, I'd been too mad at Daddy forbidding me from marrying Joe to stop and think before I repeated, "For better, for worse, for richer, for poorer, in sickness and health, till death do us part." I realized I was twirling my wedding ring on my finger, the wedding ring engraved with "From Joe" on the inside. He had a matching one that said, "From Lilly."

For whatever reason I'd sworn, I'd sworn it.

Which meant the least, the very least I could be expected to do, was go find out if Joe was dead or alive. Because Daddy had always said a man or a woman was only as good as the oaths he or she kept. That everything else—money, fame, social importance or lack thereof—was just window dressing. Only your word mattered. And I'd given my word.

And besides—

And besides, despite Joe's frequent daydreaming of finding something else to do, and the way he could worry me with his strange impulses that didn't take in account we had to earn a living, in a way I couldn't explain, he'd become a part of me: someone I couldn't imagine living without. We were linked. One thing. One being.

Call it love, if you wish. It might very well be that. In our time, no one gave love much credence and the words "I love you" could only be uttered for comedic effect, as though the idea of loving another human had become something quaint and belonging in the unenlightened past of the species. But I'd once read that loving someone meant you cared more for their well-being than your own. And if that was the case, I did love Joe.

A thought crossed my mind that perhaps it was Joe's lack of background that had set off Daddy's alarms, enough to step in. But it didn't matter. Not really, not anymore.

The Lilly Gilden who had thought Daddy was being a meany and she must contravene his orders in the most visible and irrevocable way possible was gone. Heck, the Lilly Aster who thought that people could be trusted to be more or less as they presented, had burned away like an illusion, in the last day.

All that was left now was the word I'd given and—yes—the love I still felt for Joe. It was my job to recover him.

Now. "I still have to go," I said.

Jim nodded. "Right, but remember these faces. It could be the difference between life and death."

Just before I left the ship, Jim handed me something, slipped almost furtively into my hand, as though he were afraid I'd react badly to it.

"What?" I said, eyebrows rising, as I opened my palm and saw a stud earring, surmounted by a small ruby.

“Squeeze it between your fingers if you need help. I don’t know how much or what type I can get you, but I will try. For...for you and Joe, I will try.”

I nodded, though I couldn’t imagine what James Brighton could do to help me if I were in real trouble. But then again, until today Jim wouldn’t be one of my top five people to call if I needed to change my appearance and perhaps disappear.

So—

I nodded and got out of the space bordello, stepping lightly through the airlock and down the three bright red steps into the dangerous world of Elysium.

Come Into My Parlor

The place we landed in Elysium was not at all like the arid region where Joe and I had set down.

Leaving the travelling bordello, I found myself in the middle of a bustling spaceport. And leaving the spaceport, I found I was in the middle of a bustling city.

This was Plaso, one of the largest cities in Elysium. Though the nature of the world was also immediately obvious upon exiting the spaceport.

The street I found myself in was filled with people, vehicles, and small stands of food vendors. But no one seemed to be hurrying anywhere in particular. And there was no discernible fashion trend to what people wore.

The only thing you could say was that all clothes were colorful, but you could find anything from clothes like the ones I'd seen in the Rhodes mersi, all the way to one-pieces in various states of preservation.

Also, I'd made an assumption that everyone here would look old, since the place was aimed at people living out their last few decades.

This was stupid, because of course the ability to look young far outstripped our ability to regen and rejuv the old. There were treatments and surgeries that kept you looking young until the end. Though mostly people either did not have the money, or simply didn't bother.

Most people simply didn't bother here, either, but the panoply of ages presented still ranged from mid-twenties to late two-hundreds. Although if you looked carefully at those who presented as mid-twenties, you could sometimes catch something that cracked the illusion. People moved slower and more deliberately than they would have at that age.

Of course, other people seemed young in all respects, and I reminded myself this place attracted a lot of service personnel. Androids couldn't do everything.

Just as I thought that I'd been standing on the pavement for a long time, a flying car stopped in front of me. Took me a second to realize it was a car-for-hire and either automated or remote-controlled from a central location.

A mechanical voice emerged from it: "Madam? Does Madam wish to go anywhere?"

I had, or rather Jim had, provided myself with gems containing enough credit to my persona for this type of thing.

Yes, it was possible that someone was watching, that they knew who I was, that they'd sent this vehicle to capture me. But it wasn't likely. After all, we'd gone a long, long way to manage both my transformation, and my landing in this would-be anonymous ship, in an unexpected port.

And if I refused transport and insisted on walking the—must be ten miles—to the home where Valli Arana lived, I would soon become more conspicuous than I wished to be.

I smiled and said, "Yes." Having studied the map of the area, and the streets around the home, as well as all nearby landmarks, I climbed aboard and said, "I'd like to be taken to the Luxor." The Luxor was a hotel about two blocks from the home Joe had visited. Or was supposed to have visited.

The car took off, giving me a moment of panic with how fast and how unerringly it flew. But of course, that was nonsense. Automated or controlled, the car would fly true. After all, time was quite literally money in this case.

It seemed to avoid oncoming traffic unerringly, as well as turning suddenly at corners, as though it had been notified of a shorter way to the target. All of this bespoke a world-net, I would guess.

Before I had too much time to think, it had lowered in the parking lot of the Luxor, which was, as is mostly the case, on the roof, and was giving me the price in a list of currencies. "That will be 5 lyrs, 15 Duros, 100 Midins, 465 pagika..." It continued listing equivalences, while I inserted the gem into the slot in front of my seat and selected Lyr and 6, because having travelled with Daddy, I knew that one always tipped, even automated systems. Someone, a dispatcher or a maintenance man, would do his job better for that tip.

The voice stopped mid-word, I think in listing "A million Gdurek," and had that curious type of hiccup a mechanical voice gives when changing suddenly. "Thank you, honored Madame," it said, and then the door opened, and I scooted out.

The Luxor had—because of course it had—both elevators and anti-grav wells. What it didn't have was stairs.

Even before the current situation, I was paranoid enough that I didn't like either of the options available. Now, perhaps that wasn't strictly paranoia. After all, I'd grown up as the only daughter of a very rich man, a risk for kidnapping and holding for ransom, not to mention other things. Which meant I'd been taught to mind my security and keep an eye out for possible attackers or kidnappers. I don't need to explain why elevators made me suspicious. Grav wells, on the other hand, only made me uncomfortable because I could imagine all too well their polarity being reversed.

This time, walking across the parking lot and taking the grav well down, I had to tell myself that it didn't matter this time. Or at least it shouldn't matter, since no one knew who I was. Or at least I hoped no one knew. Because if they did, then my problems were much bigger than the possibility of dying crushed as a grav well was reversed.

Sure, it was possible they'd cracked Joe's mind like an egg and had gotten a hold of his fascination with Rhodes, and maybe even of what Stella in the modified game looked like. But it wasn't likely. It had been too short a time between Joe leaving and the borg showing up at my door.

In my mind I could imagine Jim shaking his head and saying, "You don't know Ufraglio." But that was probably my paranoia speaking.

I made it, from floor to floor of the Luxor on the grav well without incident, and was left in the lobby, a vast space ornamented with every possible bad idea of rococo from the Earth and every other world since.

Stepping away from the grav well, I noted that the ceiling was choc-a-block with chubby gilded angels reposing amid improbably immense gold leaves.

More of the same surrounded the front door in an arch, to the point that it was almost a relief to emerge on the undecorated street, amid towering glass buildings.

I hurried towards the home where Arana lived.

Blue Heights was in a glass tower, of course, blue almost by necessity.

Inside the front door, it might have been a high-class hotel, filled with various sofas arranged around tables, in conversation groups.

Around them sat people who, again, looked like all ages, talking animatedly.

Instinct, or the practice of decades, took over, and I headed for the desk with three smiling young ladies behind it.

"I am here to see Ms. Valli Arana," I said. "I work for the magazine Galactic PI, and my editor has called to arrange it."

Yes, there really was such a magazine. Yes, Jim had somehow arranged for credentials for me. And yes, they had me listed as a reporter. And they had called about an interview of Ms. Arana about being one of the women pioneers in the field to have a multi-world license.

The beautiful woman who had stepped forward to attend me consulted something beneath the top of the counter, probably an embedded holo, and said, "Oh yes. Today, at 12, right? Let me give you directions."

The fact she gave me directions, complex though they were, reassured me to some extent, because there was no way that if I were suspected of underhanded intentions, they would let me go traipsing in alone.

Getting to Ms. Arana's room—or rather, apartment, as they called it—was uneventful, though I noted the pleasing nature of the surroundings. There were stairs up to the fifth floor, where she was located, and on the fifth floor, the hallways were just curved and wide enough to seem more like they'd grown in place than been carefully planned.

There were also plants, and the sort of white, immaculate statuary one associated—apparently erroneously, if some of the articles Joe had read to me were true—with Earth's ancient history. At any rate, white or not, I don't think anyone in Earth's ancient history had sculpted or distributed pictures of hippopotami in tutu skirts, for decoration or otherwise. But that wasn't even the strangest one in these hallways. By the time I got to the statue of the giraffe and the frog in romantic embrace, I decided someone was trying for whimsy.

Ms. Arana's apartment, to which I was admitted by a maid wearing clothing that could in fact be straight out of Rhodes, looked like any apartment in Father's set.

Ms. Arana...

All right, my first thought was whether Joe had been fooled. Because how could he be?

Ms. Arana was a beautiful, fluffy-haired older woman, sitting in a wheelchair. And again, I ask you, was Joe fooled? And how could he be?

Because dear Lord, no one had used wheelchairs for at least a thousand years. Regeneration and other interventions aside, there were anti-grav devices of various descriptions, including these ankle-bracelets you could wear, that allowed you to walk—or run—just above the floor, with other bracelets on your legs and thighs that allowed you to move your legs in coordination. One of Father's friends who had lost his ability to walk in a non-regen-solvable way in some kind of sport accident wore those, and no one could tell he even had a problem, unless they looked very closely at the fact that his feet never touched the ground.

But let's suppose you're poor and can't possibly afford that kind of thing. I'll confess I had no idea how much those cost. Okay, if that was your situation, you'd probably not be in Elysium.

There was still that standby of family dramas in every mersi I'd ever watched: anti-grav platforms, where the invalid sat on one, and floated above the ground, able to move this way or that with an inclination of the body. At least according to the mersis, those were the standby for every class.

But truly, it wasn't even normal to have someone lose the ability to use their legs. Most, if not all injuries, could be fixed.

So, a wheelchair raised my hackles and my suspicions. Actually, the whole tableau did.

The sweet, fluffy-haired old lady, in an extravagantly embroidered blouse in pastel tones, with a pastel blanket over her legs, sitting in a wheelchair. It was either completely wrong or altogether too perfect, and frankly I didn't trust either of those.

Surely Joe would have seen that. If this was the person he'd seen.

I introduced myself, reminded her of the interview, and she smiled, and spoke in a sweet reedy voice, telling me that I was very welcome. That she'd been waiting for me.

It occurred to me that if there were anything wrong with this scenario, Joe would have noticed it. After all, he was far more experienced than I. Then I thought he quite often missed obvious things, particularly if there was a female involved.

Of course, it could be an affectation. The very rich could afford whatever affectations struck their fancy, after all, and a wheelchair wouldn't be the worst of it.

But I was on my guard as I responded that it was lovely to see her, and started asking the questions I'd prepared.

Being on my guard helped when she came out of the chair at me, springing forward with the movement of someone a hundred years younger. That's the only explanation I have for why she failed to catch me. And why Joe— Well, never mind that.

Jim had given me a weapon, something like the zapper Joe had left with me. Don't ask me why I didn't use it. In retrospect, I think it was residual fear of seriously hurting or killing a human being. As Arana came at me, instead, I grabbed hold of the statue on the nearest pedestal and hit her over the head, hard. Yes, I do realize that could also hurt a human being, but it seemed less serious somehow.

It caught her sideways, and slightly upward, but apparently all the hypno I'd done to move properly in this form worked. She made a sound like a sigh and went down.

I could have left then. Perhaps I *should* have left then. Except that the wheelchair still confused me.

Question: if you're going to try to jump someone, why use an artifact that's going to stick out and put the person on her guard? The only thing I could imagine is that they needed something relatively mobile and not electronically wired to cover something.

Although I want to point out I didn't consciously have that thought. I just took two steps forward and kicked at the chair, which uncovered an old-fashioned trapdoor in the floor. And I realized I'd guessed it would be there when it failed to surprise me.

Which was part of the strangeness about this whole thing. I was sensing for my own reactions to things, surprised at them, as though I were watching someone else. I wondered if it was the effect of the hypnotics to turn me into...well, to make me move like Stella. It was as if something had split in my consciousness.

I watched myself pull the trapdoor up, staying out of the way, in case lasers shot out of it or something, like in a bad mersi.

When nothing happened, I neared. There was a chemical smell from down there. It was a round tunnel, with spiral stairs going down. Molded, quite modern stairs, and I felt a frisson of surprise. For some reason, probably years and years of entertainment, I had imagined it would be a tight round pipe, with metal bars on the side, to climb down, hand over hand.

I didn't want to go down there. Look, I'm not completely stupid. Going down a narrow access point was stupid. Also, it was dark, and it smelled like when you use acid to clean stone or metal. But apparently my body—or whatever of Stella they'd implanted in me—or perhaps simply a need to know what had happened to Joe overtook my rational thought, and pushed me, step by step, carefully, down the stairs.

It wasn't dark the very first few steps, because there was light from above, but after that darkness increased with every single step down. As it would. Unlike most modern construction, light didn't come on in response to my movement.

When I was only far enough in, that I could reach up and grab for the trapdoor, I did so, and pulled it shut after me. Better if someone coming into the room didn't immediately know which way I'd gone, right? I wished I could roll the wheelchair back over the trapdoor, but I was all out of kinetic powers.

As it was, my fingers scrabbled at the trapdoor bottom, before I managed to grab the barest of protrusions, a bit of the material that had pooled, and pull it down. It fell down and bounced, and then I pulled again, hoping it was enough to hide the opening from anyone entering the room who didn't know the trapdoor was there.

Which left me trapped in the absolute dark, with a smell of acid. For some reason, a memory of a lullaby my father used to sing for me came to mind: "In Elfenheim where the princess lives, there are no fears or monsters—" But I was a long way from Elfenheim. I'd left of my own free will, and Joe needed me to be strong.

The tip of my foot felt the edge of each step, as I went down, while my hand ran along the wall, keeping me on track, as I followed the spiral down, down, down.

Finally, the foot extended found no edge, and I leaned against the wall, and wondered if I should turn on one of the many implements on me that might produce a light to help me see where I'd got to.

Before I could, my eyes got used to the dark, and I found there was some light. Not a lot. It came from number displays on some apparatus, and the soft green glow of another.

I remained still, against the wall, and looked around.

It was a lab of some sort, I think. Like the tunnel that had brought me down here, it was a round opening lined with some poured, smooth material that looked like glass. Black glass. Against the walls were various machines, some with displays that showed numbers, and, near me, but on the other side of the staircase, a lot of vats, from which other chemical smells than the pervading one exuded.

In the center of the room was a vast table, with a lot of implements I didn't understand. I couldn't see it clearly, beyond the bulk and vague shape. But it smelled...of blood.

I shuddered and felt my teeth hit together, and then—

I heard footsteps. My eyes followed in the direction of the sound, and I realized there was a space in the wall between two apparatus of unknown function, and that there was a vague outline that might be a door.

A frantic look around disclosed, behind the nearest bank of apparatus, a space just barely large enough to hide me. I thought that it probably would be too hot, or electrocute me or something, as the machinery turned on, but it didn't matter. I might be wearing Stella D'Or's appearance, but I wasn't Stella. I wasn't going to shoot first and ask questions later. Heck, I might not be able to shoot at all.

I dove sideways, finding there was just enough space for me to lie down still, between apparatus and wall. The machinery on the back was smooth and felt cool to the touch, like glass or diamond. One of them vibrated very slightly, kind of what you'd expect from a cleaning system or some other unobtrusive machine.

Other than that, there were no obstacles there. Just barely enough space for me to lie down, holding my breath.

Now I realized there were two sets of footsteps, and also—voices.

For a moment the voices were indistinct. Just clear enough that I could hear emotions and inflections, but not words. As they got nearer, I realized it was two people arguing, and blinked.

But I still couldn't understand the words and had a brief moment of panic I wouldn't understand the language at all. Unlikely, in a way, since my education had included a modicum of modern language, and an implanted chip that could discern and translate the rest.

That must be what activated, because I suddenly could understand the discussion, though I still didn't have any idea what the language was.

"—still alive?"

"Yes, impossible though it seems. It's like he refuses to die. I've never heard of [untranslatable] not killing immediately. He must be made of something indestructible."

"I guess, but it is terribly inconvenient."

I tried to keep my breathing even and low, but my heart was beating so loudly that I barely heard the words through it. I had no idea who "he" might be, but was seized with the unbearable hope that it might be Joe, that Joe would in fact still be alive. The need to be with him, to touch him, was so great that I could almost feel it. My arms around his neck, his lips on mine.

I heard, in memory, as James said that he hadn't been able to find a background for Joe, but that didn't matter. Not at all. None of it mattered, provided I could be with him again. I knew precisely who he was. He was my husband. My other half. The rest was academic. And after this, if I could just get him back in one piece, I was going to find a way for both of us to run away to Far Itravine and be beach bums and raise a passel of children. If needed, I'd storm Elfenheim, and demand money from Father, whether he wanted to give it or not. Didn't care. As long as I got Joe back, I could do anything. Anything at all.

I realized they were still talking. The voices were masculine, and though the chip was bravely laboring to translate whatever they were saying, it was to my purpose nothing, because I couldn't really understand it. It was a series of numbers, mentions of name, none of them names I knew, though in the middle, pronounced with much élan, as though it were a place of some note, was "Ufraglio." Which, of course, now and forever carried an unsavory connotation in my mind.

"And the man's wife hasn't come?" the first man asked. "With the borg?"

This got my heart going fast again, because surely it must be Joe that refused to die. Good man. He would live till I rescued him. He would live with me.

"What? The Asters? No. Well, no one can find them. She seems to have disappeared. We never expected her to take off in the face of a threat to bomb her."

"Little rich girl is made of tougher stuff than anyone could guess."

A dry laugh. "Yeah, you say that, but Luzend isn't going to be happy. And he isn't the forgiving kind. Unless you want to end up like Joe Aster, we'd best figure out a way to track them, and another plan that gets the authorities to do our work for us. With them and with Gulbahar Felix, too."

"Ah," the other voice answered. "I can't end up like Joe Aster. They couldn't be sure I'd survive the borging, and even if I did, the dexterity would be too iffy to operate what they expect."

I thought I'd screamed. There was a sound like a scream or an explosion, and it took me a moment to realize it had been only inside my mind. And the two out there were still speaking. "Well, you know, the bastard took it well. I mean, being fast processed and awakened, I thought he'd be non-functional."

"If he'd been non-functional, we'd both be dead."

"Sure. Of course, he seemed somewhat confused about who he was—"

I was cold, cold as hell. Shaking, at least inside, if not externally. And my cheeks were wet, the tears running meanderingly, down my cheek and dripping to the polished floor. Why was there no dust here? They must have automated machines. Thoughts of being found, of machines, cleaning and cataloguing my position, disturbed me, but everything was detached, distant, as though it were happening to someone else, far, far away.

They were rattling numbers again, and then one said, "I guess there's nothing more we can do there. Hey, want some dinner?"

And then the lights went off, and the voices were receding. And I was lying there, shaking, wondering if I was in fact alive, and if it mattered.

Joe had been the borg. Joe was borged. A forbidden being, who would bring death to anyone who failed to turn him in. He was lost to me. There would be no Far Itravine, no time for us, no hope for maybe a few kids. There would be...

The door closed; footsteps faded. I don't know how long I laid there, unable to convince myself to move. Honestly, when I did move, it was as if it weren't me at all. Just the body, sliding slowly up, looking for a way to stand, when I was lying on my side with no space to turn.

The hand I put out for balance found a small object on the floor, and toyed with it, before I managed to pull myself up a little more, holding the object, and then more and more, till I was standing, behind the machinery, panting. The object was a ring, and I slid it onto my thumb—it was too big for any other finger—thinking I could figure it out later.

Figure what out? There was nothing to figure out. Joe was...well, not dead. But perhaps worse than dead.

And Uncle Gul... They had tried to kill Uncle Gul with something, but— He was still alive? Well, at least that was good news and I—

A cavalcade of feet down the stairs. A voice calling. "Myrt?"

Other voices, confusion. And steps fast, fast, fast down the stairway. Many steps. Many feet.

"Stop. Ms. D'Or? Stop. You can't get away."

Well, fine and dandy. I couldn't? Well, they could take that and fold it all in corners, because I definitely was going to.

I plunged blindly through the lab, hit my hip on the table, backtracked instinctively, ran towards the door, opened it into a well-lit hallway half-expecting someone to stop me. But the sounds were still behind me, and I was running, full force.

Running. My hands in front of me. Screaming.

Ahead of me were two middle-aged men in bodysuits, the kind worn by lab workers or laborers. They were probably the ones who had been talking in the lab. I didn't pause, and pushed between them, and continued running.

I heard surprised exclamations and thought they'd probably join the chase, but I don't know if they did. There were other screams and sounds behind me, and then, suddenly, I came to another staircase, and ran up, fast. No, I had no idea where I was running, just that I must get away from pursuit, which was right behind me.

A door in front of me got pushed, and I emerged, panting, into what looked like an empty office.

The pursuers were close enough. I, myself, had no idea what to do, but something in the back brain whispered that if I continued running, I'd never stop. The windows were permanently shut. The kind that don't open.

I rolled under a desk, and made myself as small as I could. The desk was the kind that had full panels side and front, and I squeezed towards a corner, hoping that I could hide in the shadows.

From where I was, all I could see was feet. Six pairs of feet in heavy boots emerged into the room. From the movements I got the impression they were young, and they were all massed, confused.

"Where?"

"Perhaps she's hiding here?"

"No. That would be stupid."

One of them was panting. "Who could imagine the bitch would be so fast?"

"And resourceful. She knocked the bait cold."

"Do you think she's trained? Someone sent to get us?"

"That is just what we need. Let's go."

They walked out, cautiously. I couldn't believe my luck, and that they hadn't looked under the desks, at all. But I guess if they were trying to catch me, they didn't want to delay. I could get away.

I stayed under the desk, panting, crying.

I don't remember getting out. I don't remember finding my way out. I don't know how long I waited.

I remember finding myself in an auto-cab. Which I must have called, but I don't remember. I was running on panic and despair. My mind seemed to go around in circles to the refrain of, "Joe is dead. Dead."

I gave the auto-cab the directions to the spaceport.

It wasn't till I found myself in front of the airlock to the flying bordello that I removed the ring that I'd put on my thumb. It was old-fashioned gold, a larger version of the one I wore. I hardly needed to look inside to know what it was. But I did. And there, it said: "From Lilly."

James opened the airlock. "Good God!" he said. "What happened to you?"

He pulled me inside. He gave me a glass of some liquor that tasted equal parts honey and burn.

Eventually I stopped crying and told him. “It’s Joe. The borg is Joe.”

After the End

I woke up in bed, covered up. Someone had undressed me and put me in a nightgown, and I hoped it had been me, but I was too tired to care.

Blinking at the ceiling, I tried to make sense of what I'd seen and heard. There had been a trap for me, that much was sure, but what about the rest?

This was all part of a setup to get me and Joe arrested? Well, me arrested and killed for harboring a borg, and of course, Joe killed. Borged. As good as killed. And dead as soon as any authority found him.

I still had his ring on my thumb. I must have put it back. I twirled it on my finger. And the tears had started again, but I didn't feel as though I were crying. More as though my eyes were crying, but I—

A soft knock at the door. "Lilly?"

I snuffled, because my nose was stopped up. "Stella," I said.

The door opened, and James's face appeared, a white and worried oval with wide, worried eyes. His hair was so much worse than his normal disarray that at any other time I'd have burst out laughing.

"Stella?" he said. He didn't add that he wasn't ready for me to assume an imaginary identity permanently. But the harmonics were there, in the hesitancy and the worry.

"I think it's best," I said. My voice sounded normal, only as if I had a cold, which made perfect sense, considering how long I must have been crying. "I—I think they're trying trap us. Can we go to the *35th Street*? Can we go to Joe?"

James hesitated. Then he came in, slowly, and sat on the bed. He reached for my shoulder, and squeezed it. "I'm sorry, Lilly. I'm so sorry. God, I'd give everything—"

"Yes," I said. "But can we go to Joe?"

James blinked. "You know... You remember?"

"Oh, of course. Yes. I remember." I twirled Joe's ring on my thumb. "I remember my husband has been borged. That he is a human brain trapped in a mechanical body. That his body is probably gone, chopped up and dissolved. The place smelled like acid. I remember, I realize. But he's alone in the *35th Street* and anything could be happening to him."

James didn't tell me that something would have to happen to him. That by law and mandate, and against the forfeiture of our own lives, we must kill the borg. Destroy it. Make it seem we'd never been near it.

And I didn't tell him that I couldn't let him do that. That I couldn't let anyone do that. That the borg who thought he was Nick Rhodes was the only thing I had remaining of my husband. That the brain in that cranium was all that remained of the man I'd married, and it was alive, and it was— And I'd not give it up willingly.

But somehow James understood it. Of all the friends Nick and I had, he'd been the closest, after our marriage. He'd known and been friends to both of us. And he had an intuitive understanding of humans. Had to have, or else he wouldn't have been able to make his way as an aggregator, would he? He had to know what would interest most of the people in the Galaxy and how to present it to make them interested. He had to.

"It's going to be difficult," he said. "I'll do what I can. But it's going to be very difficult. It— He'll need the synthetic blood that both feeds and sustains the borged brain. And it's hard for an individual with no criminal connections to find. Not impossible, but difficult, even for someone with links to Ufraglio. And I don't know how to keep affording it."

I nodded. I didn't know how to do it, either. I had nothing much, except the certainty that I must do it, that I must find a way. If needed, I'd impersonate Joe and solve cases. Well, of course I couldn't impersonate Joe and pretend to be him. No one would be that blind as to confuse us. But I would...could be his resourceful secretary who did all the research for him, and we could use his license, and I could keep him alive. I'd manage.

I might have been brought up and conditioned to be pretty useless and ornamental, but I had brains, and I'd figure it out. Even if I had to take as many Nick Rhodes mersies as Joe had, until I got all the techniques, all the...spirit of the thing.

It came to me, as if in a dream, even though I was perfectly awake, that Nick Rhodes had a similar arrangement with Stella.

He was disfigured. His face, behind the ceramic mask that looked somewhat like a borg's face, was a mass of scars and holes, created by infected bullets striking it, during the first worldwide war of Earth. It was said, by people talking about the show, at least, that Earth had been so impregnated with decaying human remains, that the bullets that grazed the Earth to hit the men in the trenches carried with them deadly poison, infections that couldn't be conquered. I had some vague memory, from my schooling days, that this was before humans had any idea how to fight internal infections, though I couldn't remember how many decades it would be before the discovery.

Anyway, in the mersi, Nick was disfigured and self-conscious about it, even though he had a beautiful mask behind which to hide his injuries. So, Stella was his "leg-woman."

Which didn't have anything to do with her legs and, strangely, no sexual connotations. Stella was the one who went out and saw people. If they needed to come see Nick, they were brought by Stella.

In fact, they never saw Nick, because he was behind a one-way mirror, able to observe what was passing, and what people said, but they could not see him. There must be better ways to do it with our tech. And Joe... Well, I had a good mind, but Joe was a genius.

"We'll have to bounce back via a safe harbor and change ships," James said. "*We* didn't exactly take off like you did last time, in the teeth of persecution, but they can't be utterly stupid. Surely they will put two and two together, and besides, someone might have seen you come back to the ship. We can't risk being traced. I've already done two jumps, and I've connected ahead. We're on our way to a safe place in Spinning Top system."

I had no idea where Spinning Top was, and I still don't know. There must be a million named but not really inhabited systems out there, and this is clearly one of them.

The place we approached looked like one of the many abandoned stations from the early days of schrodinger exploration. It had the brutalist grey architecture of the twenty-second Earth century.

Inside, though, unlike the peaceful farm of Paul's, it was a whirl of adventure. We docked to a port, and as soon as the chimes indicated the air pressure had equalized, went out...

And into bedlam. There were people running, lights, ships... Or at least pieces of ships.

I blinked, and realized it was a place where ships were taken apart and assembled.

A blond man in an oil-stained suit came towards us. "Brighton," he said. And then, "We have a ship for you. Not wonderful, but—it will get you two or three jumps without mishap. You said that's all you should need."

Later, we sat in a little cramped interstellar, the kind that had bunks on the wall, and only one room, the kind used by asteroid miners and other loners on their runs. A room with a fresher, two bunk beds, and two seats, right by the controls.

But we'd only be in it a couple of hours, or at least that was what James had said. He was working the controls, getting us through the jumps.

"Is it...that place? Is it another of your acquaintances from Ufraglio?"

He turned and gave me a smile that was half-wince, an expression that should be impossible for a human being to wear. "You know...Paul isn't... That is. He's not that bad. He's from Ufraglio, yes, but he's another refugee from Ufraglio, someone else who got away. This station, though, that's not my acquaintance. They were not doing me a favor."

"Oh?"

"They were...*are* Joe's acquaintances. He did a job for them way back, before you knew him. I only knew about it because I had to help him with part of it. But anyway, they are grateful, and I told him we were working for Joe, and that it was vital. That poor bordello ship will be gone into parts by the end of the day. Probably by now. And they won't trace us. We'll be back to the *35th Street* in no time at all."

Well, it felt like that. Jump and jump, and jump, and then we were in the middle of nowhere, and I saw the familiar contours of the *West 35th Street.*

I could have cried. Or laughed. Or something.

I realized some portion of me, some lost, forlorn, portion of my brain expected to open the door and find myself in Joe's arms. But this was not how any of it worked, of course.

When we docked, airlock to airlock, and I emerged into the *35th Street,* there was no Joe.

There was a borg. We found him sitting at Joe's desk, in Joe's chair, reading a holo book. The cover, displayed to us as we came in, was *The Iliad* by Homer.

He turned off the holo as we came in, and the voice that came out of the perfect features with the glowing blue eyes sounded more like Joe than I remembered, but it spoke with Rhodes's terms. "Ah, Stella, you've come back. Report."

I hesitated. I was literally one step in the door, and froze like that, my right foot in front of my left, as I tried to figure out what to do.

I knew what this meant. In the Rhodes mersis, Stella had eidetic memory, and could call up the recollection of everything that had happened. She could tell the entire adventure she'd gone through, so that Nick could then reason as if he'd been there.

She was the legs, and he was the brain. She did the active part of the investigation, while he did the mental piecing together of the solution. His only active part of the investigation consisted of calling people on the phone.

The thing was, if I told Joe— Er...Rhodes about what I'd found out, would he go into some deep funk and maybe die of the shock of finding out that he was Joe Aster? And—

Some deep inner part of me said this was a way to solve the situation. I might not like it, but this would solve it, one way or another.

More importantly, if I was going to keep the borg alive, I was going to have to continue solving crimes. Which required Joe's brain.

I walked back to my desk, sat down, and reported as Stella would do.

To be fair, I was surprised at how much I remembered. I'm not eidetic. Or at least I don't think I am. But I know that Stella had trained in the ability to remember this kind of thing, and perhaps— Perhaps what they'd done to me, or perhaps even something in the mersi that Joe had modified had developed that in me.

I looked at the impassive metal face, and reported everything: absolutely everything from the moment Uncle Gul came calling.

If I was telling the borg who thought he was Rhodes something he didn't know, or something that affected him emotionally—did borgs have emotions? Had to, right? After all, the brain is the biggest repository of emotions, isn't it?—he didn't betray it.

When I was done, he didn't react for a long while. Then he put his feet back on his desk, and leaned back in his chair. I could hear the chair groaning and straining under the weight. I'd have to get him another chair. Another ship. As I understood there was machinery needed to keep the brain alive. And we wouldn't have room.

I would have thought the borg, his blue glowing eyes reflecting off the ceiling, had gone into some kind of resting state. Except this position was exactly what

Joe assumed when he was thinking. And it was, I now realized, the same that Nick assumed when thinking. I smiled a little, thinking my fan-husband had probably been imitating his fictional idol.

At length, the borg creaked out, "Alex? I mean, Jim?"

This is when I realized Jim had come in and was sitting primly against the wall, his hands on his lap, like an obedient child at school.

He was looking at the borg with full attention, and he said, "Yes?"

"I need your magic. Can you get through to Idelle Zay and Maretto Luzend? Also, Raine Chlo." He paused a moment. "I wish we could also get to Gulbahar Felix, but I suppose that's impossible."

Jim made a startled movement. "Actually," he said. "I got notice he came out of a coma at... Well, while we were in Elysium."

"Excellent," the borg said, and the words sounded like Nick, but also like something that Joe might say. "I'd like to assemble them, in holo, in here at..." He started at the ceiling a while longer, then named a universal hour, the time used for setting interworld coms, about two hours distant, ship time.

Jim opened his mouth, looked at me, then looked back at Joe.

"We'll rig something to disguise my present and inconvenient form. It should be possible to contrive a...ah... An image of my flesh-self, shouldn't it? Since this is all virtual? Harder in person."

Harder in person, I thought, but we'd undoubtedly have to do it. In time. If we survived this.

I spent the next two hours making a recording of my recollections and triple-locking them. I had an idea it might be important for reference.

Well, that's how I spent most of the time, except for the time devoted to making and consuming a sandwich, since I realized with a shock that I hadn't eaten in several hours. It seemed such a distant and unimportant need.

Joe—well, the borg, spent it applying Joe's skills with electronics to the holo unit.

When I returned from the kitchen to the office, I saw Joe sitting behind the desk. If I didn't know better, I'd have run to him and thrown myself in his arms, particularly when he smiled at me.

It was Joe's familiar smile, but there was a sadness behind the eyes. I wondered if it was a recorded Joe or something the borg was controlling. I didn't remember Joe ever smiling like that, with such terrible sweetness and sadness combined.

"I'm afraid you've made a bad bargain, my dear," he said.

I made a face. "It wasn't a bargain. And I didn't make it. It is what it is."

He inclined his head. "Can you send Jim in, and get out for a moment?"

I opened my mouth to protest.

"It's not that I don't trust you. It's that I must ask Jim what we can do to...to prevent the person who... Well, there's some things we can do, you know, but they are not—Wait. I think I have it. But we'll have to call on some of his connections. And some of mine, too. And as much as he's done for you since this started, he won't want to expose other people to possible harm."

I hesitated, but felt, suddenly and with absolute clarity, that I didn't want to make James Brighton endure more than he already had. I had a feeling he'd been skating on the thin edge of what he could tolerate and that only his loyalty to Joe and gratitude for what we'd done for him had gotten him through this.

I nodded to the borg and left the room.

I cannot give you a precise account of what I'd done while waiting for them to be done with their talk, except that I was walking back and forth between kitchen and office, and wondering how much it could cost to keep a borg alive, wondering how much of Joe remained in that mechanical body, wondering if he remembered at all, and most of all wondering what he meant to do.

That smile of infinite sadness broke my heart even in memory. Now and then I touched the ring I'd given him on our wedding day, which now sat around my thumb, a reminder of the bond between us. Was it severed? Legally Joe was dead, and the "death do us part" had come. But why did it not feel that way? He was still as attached to me as this ring around my thumb. We were still Joe-and-Lilly. There was no way to divide us. My every thought, my every action checked with him and how he might feel about them.

I didn't think I'd ever not be married to Joe, even if the borg were gone today.

Was it possible to restore a borged human?

I didn't know. I had a vague idea that since the brain contained that person's DNA, it should be possible to recreate a body and restore a brain to it. But understand among the many things I knew nothing about was science. It should be possible, but as I knew from talking to scientists in my father's home, many things that should be possible weren't, until science inexplicably took a huge leap and made other things that had seemed impossible suddenly reality.

From what I understood, even borgs were impossible, until Kyre technology had made them possible by providing truly efficient and seemingly inexhaustible batteries. But—but we still didn't know how they worked or why.

What if it were not possible to bring Joe back, either now or in the potential future of our lives? I twirled the ring on my thumb. Well, then I'd stay alive as long as I could to hide the borg and not get killed.

It was not a decision, not something I could deny or affirm. It was reality. That was all.

Somehow between the day we'd registered as married and now, we'd become one being. Even if most of him was missing, I was still his and he mine.

I allowed myself a brief shudder at the thought of how difficult it would be to keep him secret. I had no idea how to do that, and perhaps the conference tonight would be enough to undo any such chance. But it didn't matter.

It was simply reality, as much as my need for water or air.

And it being thus, there was no point in repining.

I shrugged my shoulders and went to change my clothes and get ready for the conference with the various holograms. I imagined my job would be to take notes and coordinate. At least Joe hadn't told me he didn't want me present at that, and therefore—

And therefore I'd be ready to do what I normally did, as though it were all as it had been, and perfectly normal.

I went to my room and changed into a bright red dress, embroidered with dragons, and cinched at the waist with a blue leather belt. I put on matching high heels.

Oh, yes, somehow—and I didn't remember doing so—all the clothes from the flying bordello had made it to a suitcase in our ship, and thence to my closet onboard.

It seemed a shame to have the looks that Joe had designed for me, and yet not to be dressed accordingly.

I'd have to register the change of name with Galactic records. And I supposed we should file one for Joe, as well. Possibly to some annoyance from the producers of the Nick Rhodes mersis. Or not. In the midst of all our problems, mere brand infringement seemed inconsequential, particularly since most of the worlds didn't respect brands or copyrights.

I walked lightly down the stairs.

There is a point one reaches where the future seems so absolutely bleak that the only thing to do is to ignore it and act as though everything is fine.

A Thousand Ships

And for a moment when I bounced into the office, everything would seem to be perfectly fine. In fact, if it weren't for crossing paths with Jim in the entranceway, I'd have thought I'd dreamed the whole thing. But Jim looked even more bedraggled than normal. Not exactly scared or upset, but more like he was in such deep thought that he avoided bumping against me blindly and without ever looking me in the eye.

I cast a glance at him as I opened the office door. He was headed for the stairs up to our rooms, and I chose not to question it. Whatever he was doing was something doubtlessly worked out with Joe.

Joe was in the office, and my heart caught and skipped for a moment, at seeing him there.

I knew it was a hologram, cleverly contrived to hide the form of the borg, but what it looked like, as I came in, was as though Joe stood there, leaning against his desk.

There was a smile on his face, that made me think of a phrase I'd heard used in the Rhodes mersi: "Smiling like the canary that caught the cat." His blue eyes shone with a light of mingled triumph and satisfaction.

It was the look he sometimes wore when he'd been particularly clever, particularly tricky, and achieved something that seemed impossible even to him.

He grinned at me. I wanted nothing more than to throw myself in his arms and feel him embrace me. But there was nothing there, just a metallic body. I forced myself to smile, as I slipped behind my desk. "I presume I am to take notes?" I said.

He nodded. And now there was to him a tense sense of expectation, as though waiting for something.

The something materialized shortly.

From one corner of the room there was the weird flickering I'd seen before, when we'd connected to Idelle Zay. There were bits of people and rooms showing, as the call got forwarded.

And then Idelle stood there. She wore a white dress that blew softly in the breeze and stood in front of one of the most famous beaches in Far Itravine, the one they sold pictures and holos of. From a certain unsteadiness around the edges of her image, either she was a hologram superimposed on the landscape, or the landscape a hologram behind her.

It scarcely mattered which. I didn't believe, however, that a woman who had been on the run for so long would give herself away by showing such a famous location.

As soon as the hologram formed, she smiled, and bowed slightly at Joe, then sought me out with her eyes. She had after all heard the entire story. She nodded at me, her eyes saying what she knew would be kept secret. Then she sat down on a marble bench that seemed to appear, suddenly, out of the background of waves.

At that moment another flicker occurred, next to Idelle, and—without cycling through many other people and places—Uncle Gul appeared. He looked pale. A little less cheerful, a little less expansive. He looked in fact like he'd shrunk into himself. There were dark circles around his eyes, and a look of extreme tiredness.

And yet, when he saw Idelle's holo next to him, a tentative smile appeared on his lips. "Ida!" he said.

She smiled at him in turn. For a moment her eyes softened, and she looked more human than she had before. But before she could speak, the flicker happened next to them, and there was a short woman with dark hair and dark eyes, someone I'd never seen, but who had a look I'd come to identify as Ufraglio.

She wore a severely tailored blue pantsuit, and looked displeased to be holoing in. I wondered why she'd done it, and what had worked on her to do so.

A glance at Idelle, and she pressed her lips tightly together, which for some reason made Idelle smile. I thought this would be Raine Chlo. There was something familiar about her, beyond the resemblance to Ufraglians I'd seen, but I couldn't put my finger on it.

She looked at Joe, and for a moment her mouth dropped open, as if shocked to see him at all.

And then—the flicker again, this time going through a number of flickers of other people and places, and I knew that I was looking at a secret connection being made through several other locales. I thought this would be...what was the name Joe had said? A name I'd never heard. Maretto Luzend?

But instead, though it was a Luzend who materialized, it was one I'd seen before. Or at least one I'd seen an image of. Alfion Luzend, looking older and like he'd put on a few pounds, materialized standing next to Chlo. His lips were pressed tightly together, and he looked at Joe and advanced towards him, arm extended, as though he meant to poke him.

Look, holograms can't touch. Not actually touch. And they also can't disrupt each other. Even if he should overlap with Joe, nothing would happen except a weird comingling of holograms. Okay, perhaps enough to show everyone virtually present that Joe was himself a hologram. Which would be bad enough.

As I realized this, I was surprised that Joe didn't step back, startled. Instead, he crossed his arms on his chest and smiled and said, warmly, just as if he was meeting his dearest friend in the world, "Ah, Mr. Luzend. I'm assuming our mutual friend got in touch with you. It was hardly necessary for you to be present."

Alfion stopped as if arrested in his progress and glared at Joe. "Oh, no, Mister. If you're going to spread any kind of crazy rumor about my boy, I want to know why and exactly what is going on. Because there is no way I'm going to let you roll him up just because of what he is, and who he is. Ufraglio—"

"I'm not interested in rolling up anyone," Joe said. "You could have heard quietly, without being present, but since you chose to be present, please sit. We're just waiting on Maretto to start."

Alfion looked over his shoulder and said something that wasn't picked up by the mics for the holo.

It took a few seconds, but then a flicker next to him went through the same confused succession of people and places, before someone materialized, sitting in an office chair, in a perfectly normal office.

And both the office and the person made me stop in my note-taking, as my mouth dropped open.

You see, I knew that desk very well. It was the one I'd hidden beneath, in my escape from the secret laboratory where Joe had been made into a borg.

And the person sitting at it was none other than Narkissus Humel.

Even as I responded to the shock, I saw Uncle Gul's mouth drop open, and Idelle flicker. Raine Chlo just looked peevish.

And Alfion, sitting down in a vast red leather chair that looked much like one of the bigger seats in the flying bordello, crossed his arms on his chest and gave Joe a "this should be good" look.

Joe smiled, and said, "I'd say you're all wondering why I called you together. But you all know. Or at least most of you know."

While he spoke, he rounded the desk to sit in his chair. I suspected it took knowing the truth behind the hologram to hear the chair creak and to realize that his movements were slightly wrong. It was as though he were walking just a little too stiffly, a little too artificially, and as though he took too long to sit.

But when he put his feet up on the desk and leaned back—other than my fear the chair would actually break—it was just Joe doing what he normally did.

He folded his hands together, somewhere between his chest and his stomach, and looked around, his eyes sharp and attentive, his mouth quirking a little, as though the people before him, from Humel to Zay, were a joke he just wasn't quite ready to share with all and sundry.

"So," he said. "A few weeks ago, Doctor Gulbahar Felix came to us and asked us to solve a problem."

He went over Uncle Gul's story, including the attack on Uncle Gul, when we'd been ready to throw in the towel.

I sat there tingling and fearing that he would reveal what happened to him. He didn't. It was very skillfully done. He skirted around it, by talking of a look-alike of his, whom he had hired over the years to do some investigation. This look-alike was distinguished by having had some very illegal work done so that he could not be placed on any of the DNA databases. He had reason to think from the investigations done by his lovely assistant who chose to go under the nom de guerre of Stella D'Or that his associate had been borged—sad face—and this too was a crime to be investigated.

He claimed to have sent me to Elysium, and then narrated my adventures, except of course for my having found out that Joe had been borged.

"In Ms. D'Or's narration of her adventure, I realized I knew who the murderer was." He turned towards Uncle Gul's hologram. "I had at first thought that it might be Doctor Felix's invention, an attempt to entrap me into a lethal situation, perhaps at the behest of my father-in-law, who wanted his daughter back."

I made an exclamation of shock; at the same time, I'd realized that Uncle Gul had also done the same. Uncle Gul tried to rise from his hospital bed, only for it to be patently obvious that he didn't have the strength to.

Joe waved him down, while I resumed taking notes. Realizing I'd thinned my lips, in disapproval of Joe's tactics, I forced myself to relax. No, I didn't think Uncle Gul would do any such thing, but hadn't I initially suspected him of being in the *35th Street* to take me back to Daddy's house?

"I thought the whole thing was a little too pat, and when it became clear to me that my associate had been borged, I realized that it could very well have been a trap. Only—" He shrugged. "While that explained some of the events, it didn't explain all of them.

"No, it wasn't impossible for Doctor Felix to have taken some drug so as to fake an attack against himself. Someday I'll tell you of the client in Blythemar who accidentally faked his own murder. But not right now. That wasn't my main objection. My main objection is that though Ms. Zay is an accomplished artist and a genius in her field, there is no record of her being a proficient actor, much less one who can casually drop a bombshell of a clue.

"Also, I don't think, having examined her art just before this meeting, that she would have it in her to be involved with a borging operation."

He frowned slightly. "Let's face it: there is only one in our cast of characters with enough wealth and enough power to run a borging operation. I mean, there's a handful of planets where power is concentrated enough that someone—anyone at all—could run a borging operation with impunity, and get the supplies, and more importantly, use the borgs in a manner that would bring them profit.

"And yes, Elysium is an elaborate cover for a borging operation. Doctor Felix was right about that. It is an idea only a genius could come up with.

"We're used to indigents and marginal populations being taken for borging. People who wouldn't be missed, in other words. I've often wondered how much the loss and insanity associated with the borging process comes from the populations it starts with.

"The operation in Elysium circumvents that, of course, by instead taking the merely elderly. There is a span of about forty or fifty years when, thanks to rejuv, the brain is still perfectly clear, but death is plausible. And many of the relatives of those who live in Elysium have long since forgotten their relatives exist. Or if not forgotten, they've consigned them to a sort of soft memory, as though they'd sailed to the Isles of the

Blessed, where they are, after all, perfectly happy, but not in the same...plane as their descendants. To the descendants, they're already gone, after all. People who have departed in every way. And since one of the things required—I checked—on moving to Elysium is a plan for the disposal of the body, no one is going to check the ashes, or the coffin sent home for burial for the presence of a brain.

"Although I can't prove it," Joe glared briefly at Alfion, "I have reason to believe this scheme yields brains far more competent to remain sane and effective in a borg a very long time. And that the mining operation in the Elysium system is very lucrative." He looked at Narkissus. "I must hand it to you, sir, and your genius for criminality, to create something that seamless. It was like most ideas of genius startlingly simple. To the point we're surprised no one else has thought of it before."

Humel smiled. I heard Idelle gasp. Uncle Gul didn't make any noise, but when I looked at him, he was staring at his old friend as though transfixed, like a man staring at a poisonous creature, perhaps one of the deadly serpents on Nernan.

Alfion was tapping his foot on an unseen floor, with a rhythmic sound, like a man whose patience is nearing the end.

Joe smiled.

"Then I wondered if it was Ms. Chlo's doing, perhaps an attempt to destroy those she thought were responsible for the failure of her marriage to Narkissus Humel, or to give him his birth name, Maretto Luzend. But while she is deep in the borging operation, and in fact responsible for its day-to-day running, I don't think she would want to bring attention to it by using it to dispose of my double, or indeed, to exert such revenge on Dr. Felix.

"In fact, the more I looked at it, the more it became obvious that none of it made sense. For a while I despaired of bringing it all together and was sure that I must quit.

"If Dr. Felix was lying, to what end? And if he wasn't lying, why had someone brought him to Elysium, seemingly with the purpose of sending him into the sun in his ship? If it was someone involved with the borging operation in Elysium, why call attention to it? Could they be sure that nothing at all would give away why he had gone there, or his suspicions of the disappearance of his friend, Dr. Humel?

"And in fact, as I became sure that Dr. Humel, as he was, was very much alive, his history and DNA having undergone the sort of clean-up that the expected heir of an Ufraglio dynasty undergoes, and his disappearance being planned, why would he—if it was him—call attention to his disappearance? It made no sense."

Alfion made a sound like "pah," and the tapping of his foot accelerated.

"In fact," Joe continued, getting up and walking around his desk to stand in front of it, much in the same position as he'd stood when I'd come in, leaning on his desk, insouciant, like he had not a care in the world. "I might never have pieced it together, except for something Ms. Zay said. And because I was reading a book today."

"It is a very old book some of you might have heard of, called *The Iliad*, about a woman so beautiful, she launched a thousand ships. A woman so beautiful, men went to war for her, and countless went to early graves because of her."

The audience of holograms had gone quiet now, and in the silence, Jim came into the room, and sat in a dark corner of the most distant sofa: the one against the wall. He made no sound, and none of the holograms turned to look at him. They were held by Joe, as he stood straight and made an expansive gesture. "The story called her Helen, but in the present incarnation her name is Idelle Zay."

The artist opened her lips as though to protest, then closed them with a loud snap.

"Do not dispute it, madam. It would be fatuous. You know as well as I do that you have changed people's lives many times, when you arrived on the scene. Narkissus Humel was serious about a woman called Valli Arana. She was older than he, but he was very much in love with her, until you appeared on the scene.

"I talked to her via holo before her incident with my assistant, and I found that her public records aren't quite complete. After her romance with Humel broke down—probably her last chance at a marriage that would produce children—she came to the attention of Humel's father, Mr. Alfion Luzend. After a brief affair, she bore him a child: Raine Chlo."

Raine's lips twisted in something not quite a smile, and I thought yes, that's who she reminded me of, though I couldn't have put my finger on why.

She looked like her father, not her mother. But then, she'd married her own brother! There is a legend of some twenty-first century politician who did the same, but really. Who did that?

"You see," Joe said. "I think Ms. Zay and definitely my assistant assumed that Humel's divorce from her, and his taking of Ms. Chlo, was Ufraglio calling back.

"After all, it is a known fact that Ufraglio never lets its sons or daughters fly entirely free." He looked around and carefully avoided catching Jim's eye. At any rate, Jim had joined his hands in his lap, and was looking intently down at them, as though they could tell him something he didn't know before.

"But they were wrong. You see, it was Raine Chlo who had left Ufraglio entirely, who was called back. Back to be the pretend wife of Narkissus Humel, and to bring to life his dream of the perfect borging operation. After a few decades of pretend marriage, they parted. He was officially dead, and perfectly safe to assume the leadership of the Luzend family, which Mr. Alfion, tired of the responsibilities of rank, was ready to relinquish. You could say in a way setting up the borging operation was Mr. Humel's master work, his proof of having come of age.

"And they should have gotten away with it.

"Except that Narkissus couldn't let go of his Helen. He thought he could. He even, in a moment of altruism, divorced her and cut his ties with her, to keep her clear of his criminal involvements. In fact, he 'married' Chlo simply to keep Idelle Zay out of the whole affair and out of the orbit of Ufraglio altogether.

"And here we come to the fact that Dr. Felix did lie to me."

Uncle Gul sputtered.

"No, sir. I don't mean you lied to me about the events in Elysium or even your concern for Mister— Sorry, Dr. Humel. I mean you lied to me when you said you hadn't seen Ms. Zay since she parted ways with Dr. Humel.

"You had in fact met with her several times, and you were considering a marriage contract. In fact, it was Ms. Zay and not any devotion to academic life that kept you from forming any other contract."

Uncle Gul reddened and shrugged. Idelle Zay smiled. I took this to mean that Joe was right.

"And that was the problem," Joe said. "You see, Humel could give his Helen up. But he could not, would not, let her go to another, particularly not to the already famous, rich, and definitely not criminal Gulbahar Felix.

"So, he set up an elaborate trap, so he could kill both of them—by having them borged. I suppose in his deranged, jealous mind, the best revenge would be for both of them to live on as borgs for a long time, side by side, but unable to make anything of their love, nor release the other one from his or her prison."

Humel had gone white and just sat there.

"You see," Joe said, turning to Alfion. "There's only one thing that makes a clever man a complete idiot. I don't know what he told Ms. Chlo, but I expect he told her these people had found out about the operation and had to be disposed of. And she complied, but reluctantly. I'm fairly sure she wasn't directly involved, but let him take control under the belief it had to be done.

"She didn't realize he was running under the power of his fatuous conceit and jealousy and was no longer rational. Who knows how many people he would have trapped, if it hadn't been for Ms. D'Or's brave discovery? Probably a lot of them, until the whole operation became known and obvious and ensnared her in its discovery."

"I told him," Chlo erupted. "I told him we could not continue without—"

She stopped as Narkissus stood up shouting, "Shut up, shut up, shut up."

Alfion gestured to someone off-camera, and suddenly Narkissus's holo went out.

The Luzend patriarch glared. "How did you know? What gave him away?"

"He wasn't thinking," Joe said. "Not in any sense of the word. You see, he set out to entrap two specific people, and do it in a way that left his fingerprints all over the event. While he didn't say anything specific, he said enough to give an old friend and the woman who had been married to him for decades the impression he was in danger. You can't do that, unless you are the man who knows the victims intimately.

"That alone had made me sure that Humel wasn't dead. The research I did afterwards only confirmed what I already suspected. But when Ms. Zay said he'd sent her a similar letter, I was sure that it was Humel behind it. The reason was obvious, since Uncle Gul had given enough hints for me to realize he was madly in love with her. Besides, only one thing could have caused him to try such a ridiculous ploy. Though he doubtlessly thought himself very clever for not being explicit on his letters." He looked at Alfion. "Considering his vulnerability, you might not wish to give him control of—"

Alfion nodded. "Don't worry about him. He's gone."

"The other thing I hesitate to mention," Joe said, "is that I can't allow the borging operation to continue. I have made the appropriate—"

Alfion made a gesture, and Chlo got up. In the background I could hear screams, and sounds of battle. Her holo winked out.

Alfion glared, and then he too vanished.

Leaving us with Idelle and Uncle Gul. Who smiled, and tried to reach for each other through the hologram, managing only an unholy mingling of their images.

"I shall be at your bedside in less than a day," she told him.

"I should be on my feet in less than that," Uncle Gul said, and I suspected he was boasting.

Later, we received a very large transfer of funds from Uncle Gul. There was a note with it, which I didn't apprise Joe of. It said, "Thank you. I owe you more than my life. You may call on me for any favor you may need. PS: I know Joe Aster never had a double. If you need or can use my or Idelle's help to hide or do whatever you wish, let me know."

We let him know. In addition to the fee, he arranged, via a network of connections that I suspected included Jim for a better and larger version of the *West 35th Street*, one that allowed us to have life-support for the borg.

And it turned out Nick Rhodes was not an actual trademark, being the name of five citizens of five different worlds. Joe changing his legal name to Nick Rhodes as I changed mine to Stella D'Or would be viewed by most as a publicity stunt. As would be the fact that Joe never met with or touched a client, and only received clients from behind a privacy screen.

What Joe remembered of who he was varied. Half the time he really thought he was Nick. The other half... The other half broke my heart, as I could not touch him or hold him. He was alive, in a way, or at least his mind and memory was. But he was locked in such a form that made him more distant to me than the twentieth century of old Earth.

Which is where I found myself walking, on an afternoon after we had finished the case. All was quiet in our ship, and Joe was doing whatever borgs do while their synthetic blood is cleansed by very expensive machinery.

We'd brought the mersi unit aboard the new ship, with all of Joe's programing in it. It was in my room. A borg wouldn't even fit in it.

That afternoon, I got in and closed the clamshell, and found myself walking the rain-slickened, glistening streets of ancient New York.

Up the steps, and into the door of the old brownstone. Loup Armel opened the door, but something in my face must have given him warning not to speak.

I did not hand him my coat and I did not remove my hat. Instead, I walked into the office, where Nick sat behind his desk.

He got up, as though alarmed by my approach, and I walked around his desk, and up to him.

Without a word, I lifted the beautiful porcelain mask that covered his face.

Beneath, there was not the horribly disfigured, scarred flesh I'd been led to expect from the backstory of Nick Rhodes.

There was nothing but Joe's face.

Surprised, a little scared, he blinked at me in confusion.

I tossed the porcelain mask on the desk and flowed into his arms. I laid my head against the scratchy woolen fabric of his suit and cried.

Slowly, he put his arms around me. Joe's arms, enveloping and strong.

It was an illusion. I knew it was. But it was all the physical contact I could have with the man I'd loved and lost.

About Author

Sarah was born (and raised)in Porto, Portugal, where at the age of eight she decided she wanted to live in Denver and be a writer.

No, she has no idea whatsoever why Denver. Her understanding of the world, at the time, might be judged by the fact that she thought Denver was by the sea.

At any rate, having married a mathematician from Connecticut, she made her way to Denver in her late twenties.

She's raised two sons and a countless number of cats in the Rocky Mountains, and overall feels no need to repine for the choice she made at eight.

In a writing career spanning 20 years (so far) she's become a bestseller and received two prestigious awards (Prometheus: for Darkship Thieves, and the Dragon: for Uncharted, with Kevin J. Anderson.)

She's published over 30 novels and over 150 short stories, in genres ranging from science fiction to mystery, to fantasy, to historical. At the moment, she's not written children's books, men's adventure or romance. But she makes no promises. As the mathematician has instructed her to warn "No genre is safe from her."

Also By

A. K. A. I SURE WROTE A LOT

Shifter Series:

The Small Town of Goldport Colorado is a magnet to shape shifters. At the center of the community is The George, the diner run by a panther and a dragon shifter.

Their best friend, a lion-shifter policeman often requests their help in solving local murders, even as ancient shifter organizations try to claim them.

Draw One In The Dark

Something or someone is killing shape shifters in the small mountain town of Goldport, Colorado. Kyrie Smith, a server at a local diner, is the last person to solve the mystery. Except of course for the fact that she changes into a panther and that her co-worker, Tom Ormson, who changes into a dragon, thinks he might have killed someone.

Add in a policeman who shape-shifts into a lion, a father who is suffering from remorse about how he raised his son, and a triad of dragon shape shifters on the trail of a magical object known as The Pearl of Heaven and the adventure is bound to get very exciting indeed.

Solving the crime is difficult enough, but so is -- for our characters -- trusting someone with secrets long-held.

Gentleman Takes

Family! Can't live with them and can't eat them.

Tom Ormson, owner -- with his girlfriend -- of The George, a diner in downtown Goldport, Colorado is well on his way to becoming a responsible and respectable adult, despite his rough start and the fact that he turns into a dragon.

But then the unpredictable Colorado weather, the ancient leader of a dragon triad and an even more ancient shifter-enforcer combine to destroy his home, put his diner at risk and attempt to kill him.

All this, of course, has to happen while Tom's friend, Rafiel, is trying to solve a series of murders-by-shark at the city aquarium, and Tom's newly-reconciled father is attempting to move to Denver.

Fasten your seat belts, a wild ride is about to begin.

Noah's Boy

Tom Ormson and Kyrie Smith are suffering the growing pains of young romance and young business people. Tom worries obsessively about the new fryer in the diner exploding.

As though he didn't have enough on his mind, though, life decides it's time for a sabretooth with vengeance on her mind to come to town, and for the Great Sky Dragon to try to arrange a marriage for Tom.

Meanwhile, out at the old amusement park, the one with the really good wooden roller-coaster, a series of bizarre murders is taking place.

And, as if that were not enough, Conan Lung, dragon shifter, ex-triad member and waiter extraordinaire starts his country singing career with an original song "If I Could Fly to You."

When Kyrie is kidnapped, it's all Tom can do to make sure he protects her while not eating anyone.

Sweet Alice

A Shifter Series Prequel Short Story.

Rafiel Trall is studying law enforcement, preparing to follow in the footsteps of his father and grandfather as a police officer in Goldport, when he shifts shape into a lion. Fearful of hurting his classmates, he goes back home. But at home, a crime awaits his solving. And once he solves it, he will never be the same.

Dipped, Stripped and Dead

A Dyce Dare Mystery

When she was six, Dyce Dare wanted to be a ballerina, but she couldn't stop tripping over her own feet. Then she wanted to be a lion tamer, but Fluffy, the cat, would not obey her. Which is why at the age of twenty nine she's dumpster diving, kind of. She's looking for furniture to keep her refinishing business going, because she would someday like to feed herself and her young son something better than pancakes.

Unfortunately, as has come to be her expectation, things go disastrously wrong. She finds a half melted corpse in a dumpster. This will force her to do what she never wanted to do: solve a crime.

Life is just about to get crazy... er... crazier. But at least at the end of the tunnel there might be a relationship with a very nice Police Officer.

A French Polished Murder

When Dyce Dare decides to refinish a piano as a gift for her boyfriend, Cas Wolfe, the last thing she expects is to stumble on an old letter that provides a clue to an older murder. She thinks her greatest problems in life are that her friend gave her son a toy motorcycle, and that her son has become unaccountably attached to a neurotic black cat named Pythagoras. She is not prepared for forgotten murder to reach out and threaten her and everything she loves, including her parents' mystery bookstore.

A Fatal Stain

When Dyce Dare buys a table to refinish, the last thing she expects is to find a human blood stain under the amateurish finish. Whose blood is it?

What happened to the person who bled on the table?

Helped and hindered by her fiance, Cas Wolfe, her friend Ben, her son E and an imaginary llama named Ccelly, Dyce must find the killer and the victim, before the killer finds her.

Deep Pink

Like all Private Detectives, Seamus Lebanon [Leb] Magis has often been told to go to Hell. He just never thought he'd actually have to go.

But when an old client asks him to investigate why Death Metal bands are dressing in pink – with butterfly mustache clips – and singing about puppies and kittens in a bad imitation of K-pop bands, Leb knows there's something foul in the realm of music.

When the something grows to include the woman he fell in love with in kindergarten and a missing six-year-old girl, Leb climbs into his battered Suburban and like a knight of old goes forth to do battles with the legions of Hell.

This is when things become insane.... Or perhaps in the interest of truth we should say more insane.

Witchfinder

In Avalon, where the world runs on magic, the king of Britannia appoints a witchfinder to rescue unfortunates with magical power from lands where magic is a capital crime. Or he did. But after the royal princess was kidnapped from her cradle twenty years ago, all travel to other universes has been forbidden, and the position of witchfinder abolished. Seraphim Ainsling, Duke of Darkwater, son of the last witchfinder, breaks the edict. He can't simply let people die for lack of rescue. His stubborn compassion will bring him trouble and disgrace, turmoil and danger -- and maybe, just maybe, the greatest reward of all.

www.ingramcontent.com/pod-product-compliance
Lightning Source LLC
LaVergne TN
LVHW091011080826
845145LV00003B/1222

* 9 7 8 1 6 3 0 1 1 0 2 2 2 *